"拥抱·爱"系列双语典藏读物

hugs™

stories, sayings, and scriptures to Encourage and Inspire

for Grads

毕业离歌

Jeff Walling
Leann Weiss 著
汪方挺 译

安徽科学技术出版社

HOWARD

[皖] 版贸登记号:1208543

图书在版编目(CIP)数据

拥抱·爱. 毕业离歌:英汉对照/(美)沃林(Walling,
J.)著;汪方挺译. —合肥:安徽科学技术出版社,2009.1
ISBN 978-7-5337-4263-8

Ⅰ.拥… Ⅱ.①沃…②汪… Ⅲ.①英语-汉语-对照读
物②故事-作品集-美国-现代 Ⅳ.H319.4:Ⅰ

中国版本图书馆 CIP 数据核字(2008)第 198278 号

拥抱·爱. 毕业离歌:英汉对照

(美)沃林(Walling,J.) 著 汪方挺 译

出 版 人	黄和平
责任编辑	付 莉
封面设计	朱 婧

出版发行:安徽科学技术出版社(合肥市政务文化新区圣泉路 1118 号
出版传媒广场,邮编:230071)

电 话	(0551)3533330
网 址	www.ahstp.net
E - mail	yougoubu@sina.com
经 销	新华书店
排 版	安徽事达科技贸易有限公司
印 刷	安徽江淮印务有限责任公司
开 本	787×1240 1/32
印 张	7
字 数	90 千
版 次	2009 年 1 月第 1 版 2009 年 1 月第 1 次印刷
印 数	6 000
定 价	16.00 元

给爱一个归宿
——出版者的话

身体语言是人与人之间最重要的沟通方式,而身体失语已让我们失去了很多明媚的"春天",为什么不可以给爱一个形式?现在就转身,给你爱的人一个发自内心的拥抱,你会发现,生活如此美好!

肢体的拥抱是爱的诠释,心灵的拥抱则是情感的沟通,彰显人类的乐观坚强、果敢执著与大爱无疆。也许,您对家人、朋友满怀缱绻深情却羞于表达,那就送他一本《拥抱·爱》吧。一本书,七个关于真爱的故事;一本书,一份荡涤尘埃的"心灵七日斋"。一个个叩人心扉的真实故事,一句句震撼心灵的随笔感悟,从普通人尘封许久的灵魂深处走出来,在洒满大爱阳光的温情宇宙中尽情抒写人性的光辉!

"拥抱·爱"(Hugs)系列双语典藏读物是"心灵鸡汤"的姊妹篇,安徽科学技术出版社与美国出版巨头西蒙舒斯特携手倾力打造,旨在把这套深得美国读者青睐的畅销书作为一道饕餮大餐,奉献给中国的读者朋友们。

每本书附赠CD光盘一张,纯正美语配乐朗诵,让您在天籁之音中欣赏精妙美文,学习地道发音。

世界上最遥远的距离,不是树枝无法相依,而是相互凝望的星星却没有交会的轨迹。

"拥抱·爱"系列双语典藏读物,助您倾吐真情、启迪心智、激扬人生!

一本好书一生财富,今天你拥抱了吗?

A Special Gift

for:

_____

from:

_____

date:

_____

Dedication

To my three sons,
Taylor,
Riley,&
Spencer
—who will be graduates
all too soon!

谨以此书献给我的三个儿子:
泰勒,莱利和斯宾塞
——他们都快毕业啦!

杰夫·沃琳 著
《圣经》文本由勒恩·韦思摘引

Faith Holiness Hope

目　录

Contents

Chapter 1

Holding On

①

心手相连

Live your life worthy
of the calling
you have received from me.
I know the plans I have for you.
Trust me.
I have plans to prosper you
and not to harm you,
plans to give you hope
and a future!
When you seek me with all
your heart, you'll find me.
You can count on me
to faithfully complete the
good work I started in you.

LOVE,
YOUR GOD OF PURPOSE

—from Ephesians 4:1; Jeremiah 29:11–14; Philippians 1:6

4

热爱生活吧，
别辜负我对你的期望。
我清楚，
我对你寄托了什么样的厚望。
请相信，
我的愿望是让你兴旺发达，
带给希望和明天，
而不是使你受到伤害！
当你用心寻找，
你就会找到我。
你能够
依靠我来忠实地
完成我
始于你的美好工作。

爱你的，
意念之神

——摘自：《以赛所书》4:1；《耶利米书》29:11-14；《腓力比书》1:6

Traditions can be either the links that connect one generation to the next or the shackles that hold us back from the future. Without a connection to our past, we lose part of who we are and how we are shaped through the blessings and trials we've faced. But if we cling slavishly to "how it has always been", we will lose the dreams and ideas that are the hope for tomorrow.

What part will traditions play in your life? That is one of the greatest choices you will make as you embark on this next phase of living. Learning to embrace tradition as the connection to your roots while using it as the steppingstone to your dreams is the challenge of a lifetime. As you do, you will build your own traditions to pave the road to your tomorrow.

Thank you, Lord, for the blessings of my past and the traditions that have shaped my life. Guide me as I build my own traditions and celebrate the possibilities of my future.

传统要么是世代相连的纽带，要么是阻止我

们跨向明天的枷锁。不承接过去，我们会丢失部分的自

我，以及我们在祝福和磨炼中得以塑造的本源。但是如果

我们苦苦依恋于"原来的一切"，我们就会丢失创造明

天希望的梦想。

传统在你的生活中起着什么样的作用

呢？那是你在步入下一幅生活画

卷时将做出的最伟大的

选择之一。

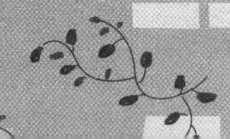

学会拥护传统,把它当做连接你的根的纽带,

同时又用它来作为你步入梦想的基石,这便成了人生的

挑战。当你这么做了以后,你将构筑起属于你的传统,为

自己的明天铺平道路。

感谢上苍用传统塑造了我们的生命,赐

予了我们幸福的过去,又引导着我们

构筑自己的传统,为未来可

能发生的事情而庆

祝。

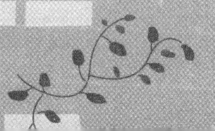

9

The past does not have to be your prison. You have a voice in your destiny. You have a say in your life. You have a choice in the path you take. Choose well and someday—generations from now—your grandchildren and great-grandchildren will thank God for the seeds you sowed.

—Max Lucado

过去 不应该成为你的羁绊。在你的命运之中，你有你的呼声；在你的生活里，你有你的发言权；在你的生活道路上，你有你的选择权。好好选择吧，将来某一天——从你们这一代起——你的孙儿和曾孙儿们将会因为你播下的种子而心存感激。

——麦克斯·卢卡多

Three weeks before
graduation day,
she made her
last stand.

离毕业典礼
　　　还有３周，
她终于表露了
　　　最后的心声。

12

Three weeks before
graduation day,
she made her
last stand.

Staying Connected

"Dad, I need to tell you something."

Jean had rehearsed the speech for hours and was determined to get through it without breaking down. She bit her lip and prepared to plow ahead when the wind blew the tassel from her mortarboard right in her face, distracting and frustrating her. Who thought up these stupid tassels anyway? Jean pondered as she adjusted the cap for the thousandth time. She wasn't much for formality: All the pomp and circumstance was so overblown. But Dad was big on tradition and ritual.

"Don't you see, Jeanie," he had often lectured her; "tradition is what holds families together. Without it you have no connection between the generations, nothing to help hold you to what came before."

And her dad definitely wanted her connected: Every family reunion at the farm in Tennessee meant a mandatory appearance by the West Coast wing of the McGee clan. Jean's dad and mom had both grown up in that small Tennessee town, and all her uncles and aunts still lived within a hour's drive of the family farm. Though her dad still called it "home", he hadn't lived there since graduating from high school. A scholarship to a big California college was too good to refuse, so he'd married Jean's mom two days after graduation and then moved to the Sunshine State, where Jean and her little brother had been born. The rest of the McGees predicted that Jean's family would lose their ties to Tennessee, but every summer that Jean could remember had included a trip to the farm and visiting all the relatives. Dad wanted them to know every cousin, aunt, and uncle by name. "This is your heritage," Dad would say when anyone complained about trips. "You have to stay connected! "

"Do you miss the farm, Dad?" Jeanie had once asked her father as they were starting the long drive back to California.

"Wouldn't you?" That was Dad—answer a question with a question. "I learned to drive a tractor, bale hay, and ride a horse on that farm. Why I remember when..." If Jeanie would just sit tight, Dad would roll through one of his stories: The time Uncle Willie had nailed his brother's hat to the farmhouse floor to teach him not to be sloppy. Or the day Aunt Mildred nearly blew up the place when the pressure cooker got too hot while she was canning peaches.

Although Jean had loved listening to those stories as a child, she had no interest in them now. It was one more sign of the gulf that had come between her and her dad: Mr. Tradition versus Miss New Age. From burning incense in her room to a tattoo on her ankle, every issue became an argument. The year she ditched the family reunion for her boyfriend's rock band's concert had nearly seen her booted from the house. Only her mom's intercession had spared her from excommunication.

But then came the graduation thing.

Jean had been adamant: She was not taking part in the ceremonies. Her friends had applauded her independent thinking. "The cap-and-gown thing is an unnecessary, outdated custom," they had agreed. But needless to say, her dad saw it differently and was ready to push the issue. Three weeks before graduation day, she made her last stand. The announcements were lying on the hall table waiting to be addressed, and her cap and gown were already hanging in the closet. She dropped the bomb at dinnertime: "I've decided I am not wearing that silly cap and gown and going through that lame ceremony," she had casually said between bites; then she had added defiantly, "And there's nothing you can do about it."

Her dad's ears had gone crimson, and her mother just held her breath. After a moment of painful silence, Jean's mother picked up her dinner, nodded to Sammy, Jean's little brother, and quietly left the dining room.

Sammy took his cue and gathered up his plate as well, saying, "I guess nobody will gripe if I eat in my room tonight." And with that the two combatants were left alone to duke it out.

Jeanie's dad began with a predictable response: "What do you think this says to your family?" When she did not respond, he continued, "Your grandmother and all the folks from back home will be here to see you graduate. It means a lot to them...and to me. Please, don't be so selfish! "

"Well, it means something to me too. I'm sorry, Dad, but I'm not backing down."

"I suppose you won't want the watch either," he had said softly.

She knew this was coming, but it made her mad that he brought it up so quickly.

"Oh, Dad, don't start with that."

"The watch" was a gold pocket watch. When her paternal grandfather had graduated from high school, the first McGee to do so, his father hadn't been able to afford a proper graduation gift, so he gave him a family heirloom, that pocket watch. That watch had been passed down from generation to generation for six decades and was always given to the eldest child at his or her graduation. Jean was the eldest McGee of her generation.

"So if I don't wear the cap and gown, I don't get the watch? Is that it?"

Her dad just shook his head, and that had been the end of the graduation conversation... until now.

The wind was getting chillier, and the ceremony was only a half-hour away. She knew if she didn't get this said now, she might never, so she started again. "Dad, this may seem strange, but I need to say this." She paused and soaked up the silence. Her father would not interrupt her.

She adjusted the cap one last time and couldn't help but grin. Here she stood in the goofy cap and gown she'd sworn she'd never wear, all ready to get her diploma in front of her relatives. But not because her father had bullied her into it. Far from it. Three days after the dinner argument, her dad had come to her room at bedtime and offered an olive branch.

"Listen, I'm tired of being mad about this. I know you're a bright girl and that you'll make your own way. Maybe it's time I let you do so." And with that, he had laid the pocket watch on her bed and walked out.

The wind blew the tassel across her eyes one more time, but she barely noticed. The tears she had fought back so fiercely now flowed freely... and she didn't care. Somehow, she kept talking.

"Dad, I want you to know why I'm doing this. It's not just because of what happened. I've thought a lot about tradition in the last two weeks. About staying connected. You never told me that it would become so much more important when...things were different."

She wiped the tears back and held out the watch.

"I'm going to carry this when I get my diploma. And one day I'm gonna give it to my child, if I'm lucky enough to have one. And I want to tell my children to stay connected to their history, their family. I want to tell them about you...I love you, Daddy. And I'm sorry."

There! She had said it. Those words had burned in her brain for the last ten days, ever since the phone call about her dad's accident and the painful meeting with her mother at the hospital. She knew she needed to say them, but her dad hadn't been able to hear them. The doctors weren't even sure if he was really alive when the ambulance brought him in: The drunk driver had hit him head-on.

"Good-bye, Daddy," she said softly as she laid a small piece of paper on her father's headstone. Then Jean turned from the grave, walked back to the car, and drove to meet the rest of family at her graduation. A gust of wind gently spun the paper on the smooth granite, as though an unseen hand was turning it around to read it: It was her graduation announcement.

一脉相承

"爸爸,我有话对您说。"

几个小时过去了,吉恩反复地诵读着演讲稿,横下心想不带磕绊地把它读下来。她咬着嘴唇,准备再念一遍,这时,风把她方帽上的流苏吹到她的脸上,分散了她的注意力,这让她感到恼火。是谁发明了这些讨厌的流苏? 吉恩一边思忖着一边第一千次地理了理帽子。她不是一个过于注重形式的人:所有的盛典仪式都太讲排场。然而爸爸却十分尊重传统和礼仪。

"你应该知道,吉恩,"他经常对她说道,"传统把家人联系在了一起,没有它,世世代代之间的联系就断了,也就没有什么东西能让你回到从前了。"

爸爸真的希望她能保持传统:每一次在田纳西农场举行的全家团聚都意味着麦格家族的西岸成员都必须出席。吉恩的爸爸妈妈双双成长于那座田纳西小镇。她的叔叔阿姨们仍然生活在那里,离家族的农场驱车仅1个小时之遥。虽然她的爸爸仍把它当做"家",但是自从高中毕业以后他就一直没有在那生活过。加利福尼亚一所大规模的学院提供的奖学金让他不忍拒绝,于是毕业后过了两天他便和吉恩的妈妈结婚了,之后就搬到了阳光明媚的加州,吉恩和她的弟弟就出生在那里。麦格家族的其他成员曾经以为吉恩一家将会与田纳西断了联系,然而,自从吉恩记事以来,他们全家每年夏天都会专程赶到农场,拜访所有的亲戚。爸爸希望他们能叫出每一位堂兄姐妹和叔叔阿姨的名字。"这是你们的世袭财产,"每当有人对旅程抱怨时爸爸都会这么说。"你们必须保持传统!"

一　脉　相　承

"您想念农场了吗,爸爸?"当他们的车踏上回加州的漫漫征途时吉恩曾经这样问起她的父亲。

"难道你不想念吗?"爸爸就是这样——喜欢用一个问题回答另一个问题。"在农场里我学会了开拖拉机、捆稻草、骑马。我总是记得那时……"如果吉恩一直坐着不动,爸爸就会向她娓娓道来自己的故事:那时候,威利叔叔曾把他兄弟的帽子钉在农场屋地板上教训他,让他不要邋遢。还有一次,米尔德里德阿姨一边烧饭一边往罐子里装桃子,烧热了的高压锅差点儿把房子都炸翻了。

还是个孩子的时候吉恩很喜欢听这些故事,然而现在她没有了兴趣。这是她和她的爸爸之间出现鸿沟的又一个迹象:传统先生对抗新生代小姐。从她在房间里点火烧香到她在脚踝处文身,每一件事都会引发一场争执。有一年,她为了参加男友的摇滚音乐会而放弃了家庭团聚,结果差点儿被逐出了家门。幸亏母亲的求情才让她躲过了一劫。

随后她毕业的日子来临了。

吉恩一直很坚决：她不想参加毕业典礼。她的朋友们为她的自由想法喝彩。"这种穿衣戴帽的事情是一种没必要的、过时的习俗。"他们附和着说。但是不用说，她爸爸的看法完全不同，而且正在筹备着这一件大事。离毕业典礼还有3周，她终于表露了最后的心声。参加典礼的来函放在厅里的桌子上等着做出回执，她的方帽和长袍也已挂进了壁橱。吃晚餐时，她扔下了炸弹："我已决定不穿戴那蠢衣蠢帽，也不去参加那种毫无意义的仪式了。"她漫不经心地一字一句地说道。接着又挑战性地补充道，"你们也别想管我。"

爸爸的脸红到了耳根，妈妈屏住了呼吸。一阵难熬的沉默过后，吉恩的妈妈端起了碗筷，朝吉恩的弟弟萨米点了点头，然后悄悄地离开了餐厅。萨米心领神会地端起盘子,说道,"今天晚上我回自己的房间吃晚饭,我想没有人会反对吧。"这样屋里就剩下两位斗士一决高低了。

爸爸打开天窗说亮话:"你知道这对全家人来说意味着什么?"她没有吱声,他继续说道,"你的祖母和所有的亲戚都将大老远地从家里赶到这儿来参加你的毕业典礼,这对他们和我来说意义深远,请不要太自私自利了!"

"哎,这对我来说也意义深远。对不起,爸爸,但是我不会改变自己的主意的。"

"我猜你也不想要那块表了,"他温和地说道。

她清楚事情会是这样的,但是让她受不了的是他这么快就提出来了。

"噢,爸爸,不要说那种话。"

"那块表"是一块金色的怀表。她的祖父是麦格家族的第一位高中毕业生。祖父毕业时,他的爸爸买不起合适的毕业礼物,于是把家里的传家宝即那块怀表送给他了。60年过去了,这块表世代相传,总是作为毕业礼物送给长子或长女。吉恩在她这一代里是麦格家族年龄最大的孩子。

"这么说如果我不穿戴那方帽和长袍,我就不能得到那块表,是这样的吗?"

她的爸爸只是摇了摇头,然后就结束了那场关于毕业典礼的谈话……直到今天。

风刮得越发凛冽了。离毕业典礼还剩半个小时。她明白如果她现在不说出来的话,也许再也没有机会说了。于是她开口道,"爸爸,也许有点奇怪,但是我必须把它说出来。"她停了停,陶醉在沉静之中。她的爸爸没有打断她。

她最后一次理了理帽子,禁不住嘻嘻地笑了。现在,她身着那套她曾经发誓永远不穿的滑稽毕业礼服站在那儿,准备当着亲戚的面接过她的毕业文凭。她现在这样做不是因为她父亲的逼迫。事情远不止这样。那天晚餐争论后的第3天,她的爸爸在就寝时分来到她的房间,递给她一支橄榄枝。

"听着,我讨厌没完没了地纠缠此事。我知道你是一个聪明的孩子,你将会走自己的路。也许到了我该放手的时候了。"说完,他把那块怀表放在她的床上,走出了房门。

风又一次把帽子上的流苏吹到她的眼前,但是她几乎没有注意到。她强忍着的眼泪现在哗哗地流淌着……她全然不顾了。不知怎么的,她滔滔不绝地开口说了起来。

"爸爸,我想让你知道我为什么这样做了,这不仅仅是因为发生了的这一切。在过去的两周里,我对于传统考虑了很多。关于沿袭传统,您从来没有告诉过我当某些事情发生了变化时,它会变得更加重要。"

她擦掉了眼泪,拿出了怀表。

"我准备带着它参加毕业典礼。将来某一天,如果我有幸有孩子的话,我要把它传给我的孩子,我要让我的孩子们保持他们历史的和家族的传统。我要对他们讲起您……我爱您,爸爸,我错了。"

啊!她终于说了出来。在过去的10天里,这些话一直在她的脑海里燃烧。10天前,她接到了电话,她父亲出了车祸,然后在医院里她十分痛心地见到了母亲。她清楚她必须说出这些话,可是那时她的父亲没法听到。当救护车把他送进医院时,医生们甚至不能确定他是否真的还活着:一位酗酒的司机迎面把他撞倒了。

"再见了,爸爸。"她轻轻地说,一边把一张小纸片放在父亲的墓石上。然后,吉恩从墓地里转过身,走向车子,匆匆赶往毕业典礼和其他的亲人会面。一阵风轻轻地吹来,转动着平滑的花岗石上的纸片,好像一只无形的手在翻转着它,念着:那是她的毕业宣言。

2

Trusting Truth

2

相信真理

Godliness has value for
all areas of your life,
holding promise
for both now and eternity.
Follow my formula
for success by growing in
diligence, faith, moral excellence,
knowledge, self-control,
perseverance, godliness,
brotherly kindness, and love.
For as long as these qualities are yours
and are increasing, you'll always
be fruitful and productive
in the equation of life.

LOVE,
YOUR CREATOR

—from 1 Timothy 4:8; 2 peter 1:4–11

虔诚的态度惠及
你生活的方方面面，
为了现在和永恒的未来，
信守你的承诺吧。
请跟随我的准则
迈向成功，
坚守勤劳、忠诚、高尚的情操，
保持热爱知识、严格自律、
坚定不移、虔诚、友爱的美德，
并不断成长。
只要你具备了这些品质，
并不断提升它们，
你就会在生命的方程中
收获成功。

爱你的

造物主

——摘自：《提摩太书》4:8;2《彼得书》1:4-11

There are voices in the world that suggest that right and wrong are passé, that notions like good and evil are fit only for children's stories. This is not so.

God has placed an economy in this universe that successful people use to guide their choices. It recognizes that right and wrong, good and evil are not arbitrary forces that change with the times. They are as constant as $2+2=4$. Learning the immutable laws of life is the greatest education one can attain.

Though the truth is not always as clear as a mathematical equation, knowing what is right and seeking to do it will never lead to a faulty answer.

Look for the constants as you walk the path of life. Memorize them as you would a chart of formulas, and they will come in handy again and again as you face the complex decisions that will make up your tomorrow.

Teach me, oh Lord, to number my days that I may gain a heart of wisdom.

世上有许多人认为,对错不过是过眼云烟,

善恶的概念也仅仅是儿童故事的素材。事实并非如

此。

在宇宙间,造物主早已作了合适的安排,使得那些成

功的人们能够做出正确的选择。它向人们昭示,对与

错,善与恶,不是随着时间的变化而变化的随意

存在力量。它们是永恒不变的等式,正如

$2+2=4$一样。懂得生活中不变的规

律乃是一个人获得的最

大教育。虽然

真理不总是像数学方程式一样清楚明了，

但是知道什么是对的并且努力地追求，我们就永远不会

被引向一个错误的答案。

在生活的道路上寻求不变的等式吧，记住它们，正

如你记住一个公式图表一样。当你要做出将会决定

你明天的复杂决定时，它们就会一次又一次地

为你所用。

啊，上帝，请告诉我何时我

才会获得一颗智慧之

心呢？

The simple basics of life—love, faith, and hope—are all we really need. We can't undo all the world's wrongs, but we can affect the corner of the world we live in if we'll just stick to the basics—the basics of life.

—Kirk Sullivan, 4HIM

爱，忠诚，期盼——这些基本的生活要素是我们真正需要的东西。我们不能消除世上所有的过错，但是，只要我们坚守这些要素——生活的基本要素，我们就能影响我们所在的世界的某个角落。

——柯克·苏利，"为了他"乐队

"If you keep doing
the same thing,
the same way,

you will keep getting
the same results."

"如果你始终
用同样的方式
做同样的事情，
你将始终得到
一样的结果。"

"If you keep doing
the same thing,
the same way,
you will keep getting
the same results."

40

By the Numbers

"Anybody home?" Shannon called as she stuck her head into room 216.

The room smelled of chalk dust and dry paper, and Shannon couldn't shake the old feeling that she should have studied harder for the test she was about to take. But there was no test today. The school year at Redlands High had officially ended almost twenty-four hours ago. And besides that, it had been two years since she had been a student in Mr. Schiller's algebra class.

Her family had moved to Redlands from Cleveland the summer before her sophomore year. Her father's transfer had been sudden, and Shannon had barely had time to say her good-byes before the moving van arrived. But if the truth were known, there weren't that many good-byes to be said. Her family's constant moves kept her friendships few and shallow.   And her older brother's athletic talents kept Shannon securely in the shadows. Buck was the star quarterback, first-string center, and ace relief pitcher—the kind of kid that high-school legends are made of.   Shannon was always "Buck's sister".   But she didn't begrudge her brother the fame; She did what most kids do in that spot: accept it quietly and look for some place she could excel.

And that's where Mr. Schiller, her algebra teacher, came into her life. Schiller was a first-generation German immigrant. Nearly seventy years old, he always dressed in a starched-white, long-sleeved shirt and a tie—the picture of efficiency and predictability. It was rumored that his father had been in the German army, but Mr. Schiller always deflected questions about his father with the same response: "That was a long time ago, today is what matters."

But there was one subject you couldn't keep him quiet about: math. He was passionate about numbers, and that passion attracted Shannon in a strange way. When Mr. Schiller talked about formulas or equations, you would think he were describing a long-lost love. Some students dubbed him the "Math Nazi", but Shannon found the elderly man to be a model teacher. His class was like another world. When you came into his classroom, it didn't matter who you were or where you were from. In room 216, the only thing that mattered was the numbers...and getting them right.

Shannon had her share of trouble getting the numbers right. She had nearly flunked two of Mr. Schiller's quizzes and was on her way to her first F in her high-school career when he asked her to stay after class one Friday.

"You don't like algebra, do you, Miss Hauptmann?" Mr. Schiller asked.

"I wouldn't say that. I just can't seem to get it."

"Oh you can get it, Miss Hauptmann. You just have

to do it by the numbers."

"I'm trying to, Mr. Schiller."

"Really. Let's just see how you are trying." He picked up the chalk and began to write on the board: $F= C+H$.

"Would you please solve this equation?" Shannon looked confused. Mr. Schiller let her stew a moment and then picked up the chalk again. "How many hours of class time have we had in algebra this semester?"

"Uh," Shannon stuttered, "I have no idea."

"Yes you do. Think about the numbers! Forty-five minutes each day, five days a week, for six weeks. How much is that?" Before Shannon could protest, he had the chalk in her hand and was guiding her through the simple calculations. $C=(45 \times 5 \times 6)/60$. She wrote the answer on the board, *22.5 hours,* and tried to hand the chalk back.

"Oh no, we are not finished yet. Now, how many hours do you give to math homework each night?" Shannon thought quietly. Mr. Schiller sat on the edge of his desk watching her, then he added, "The truth, Miss Hauptmann, will set you free."

"I guess I spend about fifteen minutes a night...on average.

"All right then, how many hours have you spent in total on math homework so far this semester?" The answer was obvious: In the first six weeks of the semester, Shannon had invested only seven and a half hours in homework.

"So the equation looks like this." Mr. Schiller wrote in broad, clear strokes on the board.

F=22.5 hours+7.5 hours

"The numbers do not lie, Miss Hauptmann. If you keep doing the same thing, the same way, you will keep getting the same results. The question is, What part of that equation do you want to change?"

"Well, I'm sure not excited about bringing home an F," Shannon responded.

"Then you must get excited about the numbers! If you want to change this F to an A, then start by changing this." Mr. Schiller circled the number of hours she had studied. "Why don't we try a little experiment, you and I. You change this 7.5 to, say, 15 hours over the next six weeks. You understand what that means?"

"I would have to double the time I spend on math every night."

"That's right! You do it by the numbers, and I will throw out those first two quiz grades, and we'll see what results you get? Deal?"

"Deal." As they shook hands, Shannon couldn't help smiling: This man was into his math. And soon, so was Shannon. She found herself more than doubling her study time and even reading ahead to the concepts that were coming up next. And Mr. schiller stoked the fires of her interest with little cryptic notes of encouragement on her homework: "The numbers don't lie! " or "Trust the numbers! "

By the end of the first semester, Shannon had a solid A in algebra.

Over the rest of that school year, Shannon made

more visits to room 216 after school, but none of them was mandatory. She would drop by just to chat—first, about math, and then, about life. Shannon found it a-mazingly easy to talk with him about her problems. He would speak persuasively of the importance of making good choices and the responsibilities of freedom. And he would always turn her problems into equations. The time she had gotten in trouble at home for lying to her moth-er he had drawn this equation: *TRUST=H+T.*

"You have lost a terrible thing," he had said, staring over the glasses that always rode nearly at the edge of his pointed nose. "You've lost the *trust* your mother had in you. When you lied to her, you destroyed the trust you had built up in your relationship."

"But how do I get that back?" Shannon asked.

"By the numbers, Shannon: *Trust* is equal to *honesty* over *time.* You must be consistent and honest with your parents over time for that trust to be regained. There is no short-cut —the equation is unchangeable."

And Mr. Schiller had been right. He had an equation

for just about everything, and they all made sense. As she grew in her respect for Mr. Schiller, she grew in her confidence in herself. While Buck received a sizable football scholarship at UCLA, Shannon had enjoyed deciding which of the four universities that were vying for her attention she would attend. Mr. Schiller even helped her to develop a chart to rate each one over a number of areas. As usual, his formula proved valuable. She would begin at Massachusetts Institute of Technology in the fall with all her tuition covered by math scholarships. She had dropped by on the last day of school to share the good news with her math mentor, but he had already left the campus. So she had gone by the next day on the chance that she might find him cleaning out his room.

"Hello, Mr. Schiller? Anybody home?"

A pair of glasses perched on a pointed nose appeared from behind the desk. "Shannon! I'm so glad you came by. Did MIT come up with the numbers?"

"Oh boy, did they—nearly 20 percent more than I had expected. Thanks for all your help, Mr. Schiller."

"Helping others is what makes life add up! "

Mr. Schiller stood up, and Shannon noticed that he had rolled up the sleeves of the old blue work shirt he was wearing. She had never before seen him so casually dressed and was about to comment on it when she noticed something on his left arm. It was a set of numbers tattooed in his flesh.

Mr. Schiller caught her gaze and quickly covered the numbers with his other hand. He turned to pick up another box of papers and carried them to a closet in the corner. Shannon stood quietly, thinking through what she had just seen. Schiller hadn't been a Nazi—he had been in a Nazi concentration camp. He was a German Jew. Now all those lectures on freedom and responsibility made so much more sense. The silence grew awkward, and it was Mr. Schiller who finally broke it.

"For a long time I hated numbers. I swore I would run from them, rid my life of them. Strange, no? I have given my life to them instead."

"No, sir. You have not given your life to numbers."

Shannon said gently. "Numbers don't mean anything. It's the people who use them that make all the difference. Mr. Schiller, I don't know what you went through to get those numbers on your arm, but you had every right to be bitter and cynical about this world."

"That is true," Mr. Schiller agreed.

"But you weren't. You chose to care for me and hundreds of other students who learned from you. You taught us more than numbers. You taught us to do it right. To be right. You know what I'm going to be majoring in at MIT?"

Mr. Schiller just shook his head.

"Math. I want to be a math teacher who changes the world by the numbers: one student at a time."

Mr. Schiller smiled as a solitary tear rolled down his cheek. "And so you will, Miss Hauptmann. And so you will."

数字背后的故事

"有人在家吗？"香农朝216房间探着头喊道。

房间里散发着粉笔灰和干纸的味道。香农一直摆脱不了心里的那个想法，觉得考试快到了，自己应该更加努力些。然而今天没有考试。差不多24小时之前，瑞德兰兹本学年的功课已经正式结束。除此之外，她也结束了席勒先生教授了两年的几何课。

上高二之前的那个夏天，香农全家从克利夫兰搬到了瑞德兰兹。父亲的这次搬迁来得很突然，她几乎没来得及说声再见便上了大篷车。但是,如果人们知道了事实真相,就不会有那么多要说的再见了。家庭的不断迁移使她的友谊变得又少又淡了。她哥哥的运动天赋才能让香农沉浸于光环之中。布克是一位明星级的橄榄球四分卫,一流的中卫和A级的替补投手———个创造高中神话的小伙子。香农不过是"布克的妹妹"。但是她并不嫉妒哥哥的荣誉。像大多数处于那种境地的孩子一样,她的态度是:平静地接受事实,寻找超越的机会。

这时,她的几何老师,席勒先生走进了她的生活。席勒先生属于第一代德国移民,近70岁高龄,总是穿着浆白色的,长袖的衬衫,打着领带—— 一副办事有效率,看上去就让人相信的模样。据说他的父亲曾参加过德国军队,但是席勒先生总是用同样的回答来避开关于他父亲的问题:"那是很久以前的事了,关键是看现在。"

然而,有一个话题你是不能让他保持平静的:数学。他对数字充满了激情,而且这种激情以一种奇怪的方式吸引了香农。当席勒先生谈起公式或方程式时,你会觉得他仿佛正在描绘一段早已丢失的爱情。一些学生给他起了个绰号叫"数学纳粹",但是香农认为这位老人是一名模范教师。他的课堂简直是另一个世界。当你走进他的教室,你就会忘了你是谁,或者来自什么地方。在216房间,唯一重要的事情就是数字……得出正确的数字。

让香农感到痛苦的就是得出正确的数字。她两次险些没有通过席勒先生的小测验,正面临着要得到她高中阶段成绩单上的第一个F。一个星期五下课之后,他把她留了下来。

"你不喜欢几何,是吗,豪普特曼小姐?"席勒先生问道。

"我没有说不喜欢,似乎就是做不对。"

"噢,你能做得对,豪普特曼小姐。你只需要通过数字就能做到。"

"我会努力的,席勒先生。"

"真的,我们只要看一看你是怎样努力的就行了。"他拿起粉笔,开始在黑板上写下:F=C+H。

"请你解出这道方程式好吗?"香农显得很迷惑。席勒先生让她苦思了片刻之后又拿起了粉笔。"这个学期我们上了多少节几何课呀?"

"呃,"香农结结巴巴地说,"我不知道。"

"不,你知道。思考一下这些数字吧! 每天45分钟,1周5天,总共6周,是多少呢? "未等香农拒绝,他已经把粉笔放到她的手上开始指导她做起了简单的运算。C=(45×5×6)/60。她在黑板上写下了答案,22.5小时,然后想把粉笔递回去。

"噢,不,我们还没算完呢。现在,算算你每天晚上花了多少时间做数学作业呢? "香农静静地思考着。席勒先生坐在桌边看着她,补充道,"豪普特曼小姐,说实话会使你解脱的。"

"我猜我一个晚上花了大约15分钟……平均。"

"好的,那么,这个学期到目前为止你在数学家庭作业上总共花了多少小时呢?"答案很明显:在这个学期前6周里,香农在数学家庭作业上仅投入了7个半小时。

"所以等式看起来似乎是这样。"席勒先生用醒目明了的笔在黑板上写道:

F=22.5小时+7.5小时

"数字不会撒谎,豪普特曼小姐。如果你始终用同样的方式做同样的事情,你将始终得到一样的结果。问题是,你想改变等式的哪个部分呢?"

"哎,反正不乐意带一个F回家,"香农回答道。

"那么你必须对数字兴奋起来!如果你想把F变成A,就必须从改变这个开始。"席勒在她计算出来的小时数上画了个圆圈。"你和我,我们来做一个小小的试验吧。比方说,在接下来的6周内你把这个7.5小时换成15小时,你知道那意味着什么吗?"

"那每天晚上我花在数学上的时间得翻倍。"

"对!从数字上开始行动吧,我将把前两次测试的成绩删掉,咱们将看到期末你最终会取得什么样的结果。成交吗?"

"成交。"他们握手的时候,香农禁不住笑了:这个人陷入了他的数学。然而不久,香农也陷入了数学。她发现自己不仅仅翻倍了学习的时间,甚至还有提前预习下节课的概念。席勒先生则不时在她的家庭作业本上附上一些鼓励性的、隐秘的小字条来煽动她兴趣的小火苗,如"数字不会撒谎!"或者"相信数字吧!"

第一个学期结束时,香农在几何上得了一个实实在在的A。

数 字 背 后 的 故 事

在那个学年余下来的时间里,香农放学后更多次地访问216房间了,但是每一次都是自愿去的。她常常只是顺道拜访一下,聊聊天——一开始谈数学,后来谈生活。香农发现,和他一起谈论,她的难题就会变得出奇的容易。他常常劝告性地提起做出正确选择的重要性以及自由之中的责任。他总是把她的问题变成公式。当她因为在家里对母亲撒谎而陷入困境后,他曾经写下过这样的公式:

TRUST=H+T

"你丢掉了件可怕的东西,"他曾经透过眼镜的上方瞪着眼说道。那副眼镜总是架在他尖尖的鼻子边缘。"你丢掉了你母亲对你的信任。当你对她撒谎时,你损失了你在你们关系中建立起来的信任。"

"但是我怎样才能挽回它呢?"香农问道。

"让数字来说话吧,香农:信任等于诚实加时间。你必须自始至终对你的父母讲诚信,这样经过一段时间信任就会恢复。没有捷径可走——等式是不可改变的。"

席勒先生是对的。他用等式表达几乎一切事情,而且都表达得很清楚。随着她对席勒先生的崇敬之情不断提升,她对自己的信心也在逐渐增强。当布克获得了加州大学洛杉矶分校提供的一笔可观的足球奖学金时,香农已经乐滋滋在4所向她抛出了绣球的大学中做着选择呢。席勒先生甚至帮她列出了一张图表,让她对这4所学校进行方方面面的比较。像往常一样,他的公式被证明很有效。她将在秋季上麻省理工学院,所有的学费由数学奖学金提供。在学期结束的最后一天,她曾经顺道去了一趟学校,想与她的数学恩师分享一下她的好消息,然而他已经离开了校园。于是第二天,她又去了一趟,指望或许在他打扫房间时碰见他。

"喂,席勒先生? 有人在家吗? "

一副架在尖尖鼻梁上的眼镜从桌子后面露了出来。"香农!你来啦,太让人高兴了。数据证实了麻省理工学院是最棒的,不是吗? "

"啊好家伙,的确如此——比我想象的超出20%。谢谢您的一切帮助,席勒先生。"

"帮助别人就是提高生命的价值!"

席勒先生站了起来。香农注意到他身穿的那件旧的蓝色工作衫的衣袖被卷了起来。以前她从来没有看见他这么随意地着装,正准备要说上几句时,突然,她注意到了他左臂上的某种东西,这是文在他身体上的一组数字。

席勒先生看见了她的眼神,飞快地用另一只手遮住了数字。他转身拿起又一盒试卷,放进角落处的一个壁橱里。香农静静地站在那儿,思索着刚刚看到的一切。席勒先生不是一位纳粹——他曾经被关押在纳粹的集中营里。他是一位德国犹太人。现在,所有那些关于自由和责任的说教都变得更加有意义了。他们陷入了可怕的沉默。最终,席勒先生开口说话了。

"在很久一段时间里,我讨厌数字。我发誓我要远离数字,把它们从我的生活中根除。觉得奇怪吗? 我却把我的一生给了它们。"

"不,先生,你没有把你的一生给了数字。"香农轻声地说道。

"数字并不意味着一切,影响一切的是使用数字的人。席勒先生,我不清楚这些数字是怎样被刻到你的手臂上的,但是,你完全有权利变得玩世不恭,对这个世界充满仇恨。"

"是的,"席勒先生同意道。

"但是您没有,您选择了关怀我和其他上百的跟你学习的学生。您教会了我们比数字更多的东西,您教会了我们正确行事。哦对了,您知道我打算在麻省理工学院专攻什么吗?"

席勒先生摇了摇头。

"数学。我想当一名数学老师,通过数字来改变世界:一次改变一位学生。"

席勒先生笑了,一颗孤独的眼泪顺着他的脸颊流了下来。"你会做到的,豪普特曼小姐,你会做好的。"

Chapter 3

Growing through Giving

3

在奉献中成长

When you feel over whelmed
and at the end of yourself,
look up and remember that
your help comes from me!
See my power perfected
in your weakness.
I am able to
abundantly stockpile you with
all grace and sufficiency
so that you will have more than enough
for every good deed I call you to.
When you love me
and are called according to
My purpose,
I cause all things to work together
for your benefit.

MY ALL-SUFFICIENT GRACE, YOUR FAITHFUL GOD

—from Psalm 121:1–2; 2 Corinthians 12:9; 9:8; Romans 8:28

当你感到不知所措，

精疲力竭的时候，

抬头看吧，

而且切记，

你的帮助来自于我！

看吧，

我的力量使你的弱点得到了美化。

我能够把所有的恩典和

足够的资源慷慨地储备于你，

让你具备极大的能量

来行使不只于

我所赐予的每一件善事上。

如果你爱我

并且遵循我的意志，

我便召集万事万物

为你的福祉效力。

我所有的恩典，
你忠实的上帝

——摘自:《诗篇》121:1-2;《哥林多书》12:9;9:8;《罗马书》8:28

Weakness is no one's goal. Strength and right are the twin companions of victory. Yet grief and loss are the ambassadors of growth and the harbingers of wisdom. They reveal what would otherwise have been hidden and bring into sharp relief the reality that is life. They provide the contrast that makes the bright days brighter, and they bring the humility that allows us to handle later victories well.

So do not despise the broken wing, the

shattered dream,   or the dashed hope. For though they bring tears and grief, they prepare you for a dream un-seen, a hope unimagined. Look behind the tragedy, and you are likely to find an opportunity to bless and be blessed. Anything less, and the pain will have been wasted. That is the definition of true tragedy.

Dear God, show me the lessons in my weakness and the   path   to   service through my pain.

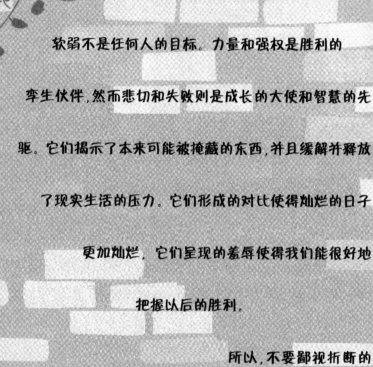

软弱不是任何人的目标。力量和强权是胜利的

孪生伙伴，然而悲切和失败则是成长的大使和智慧的先

驱。它们揭示了本来可能被掩藏的东西，并且缓解并释放

了现实生活的压力。它们形成的对比使得灿烂的日子

更加灿烂，它们呈现的羞辱使得我们能很好地

把握以后的胜利。

所以，不要鄙视折断的

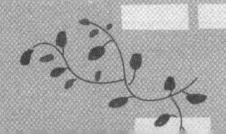

翅膀，不要不屑

破碎的梦想和即逝的希望。因为，虽然它们带

来了眼泪和悲伤，但是它们却为你看不见的梦想和没有

想到的希望做好了准备。朝悲剧的后面望去，你就有可能

发现一个祝福和被祝福的机会。缺少任何一点，痛苦

就会白白付诸东流。这是真正的悲剧。

亲爱的上帝，请揭示我的弱点

以及历经痛苦而造福世

人的道路吧。

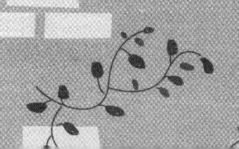

Love cures people, the ones who receive love and the ones who give it, too.

—Karl A. Menninger

爱能够疗伤，包括给予爱与接受爱的人们。

——卡尔·A.梅宁格

Sheila had figured
that if she could get
thirty pills
and take them
all at once,
that would do it.

希拉盘算着
　　如果她能收集到 30 片，
就一次性服下它们，
　　　　这样就能如愿了。

Sheila had figured
that if she could get
thirty pills
and take them
all at once,
that would do it.

Something about Mary

Sheila smiled as she pulled into the handicap parking space behind the school gym. Parking was one of the few things that had actually gotten easier since being confined to a wheelchair. She unlatched her chair from the brace that held it in front of the steering wheel of her van and rolled back onto the lift that lowered her to the sidewalk. She smiled again, thinking how second nature all this had become in just three months.

It had been a muggy morning in August when she had stepped off the curb at Harris Avenue and into the path of a Toyota truck. As usual, she had been well ahead of the rest of the girls cross-country team as they went through the daily rigors of the summer training. Only Kim Miller had been close enough to actually see the accident. "It looked like you were an angel... flying," she had told Sheila later in the hospital.

And indeed she had flown—thirty-six feet, according to the police report. The doctors called it a miracle that she had survived, and Sheila's church prayed nonstop for the first forty-eight hours that she was in the coma. Once she came to, they prayed that she would be able to run again. That prayer was not to be answered. Three of the vertebrae in Sheila's lower back had been smashed to powder. The pressure had nearly severed the spinal cord, and she had no feeling or control of the lower half of her body.

For three months she had awoken each morning praying it was all a bad dream. But soon her prayer changed: "If I can't walk again, God, let me die." But even that request went unanswered: Her heart was in good condition, and the doctors patiently assured her that she could live a "normal life"...in a wheelchair. Sheila decided she would answer her own prayer. She quietly began saving up the pain pills that the evening nurse at the rehabilitation center grudgingly gave her when she complained that she could not sleep. Sheila had figured that if she could get thirty of them and take them all at once, that would do it. Thirty days. That's all it would take.

It was on the twenty-eighth day that Mary Johnson spilled urine all over Sheila's lap.

"What are you doing! " Sheila shouted as the warm yellow liquid squirted from her "leg bag" and onto her white shorts.

"Ooooh, I am so sorry, miss. I've messed up again." Mary was trying to stop the flow of the urine, but her attempts to pull the bag away just made it squirt more.

"You idiot. Let it go, just let it go! " Sheila, swatted Mary's hands away from the bag and then pinched the end of the tube tightly. "You have to undo that strap and clamp it before you can take it off. Don't you know that?"

"I'm so sorry, ma'am, I should have waited for Mrs. Bannister to help me. Please don't say nothing," Mary's eyes pleaded. "I just started yesterday, but I ain't gonna make it. I know that."

"Hey, a little pee on the floor isn't the worst thing that can happen to a girl."

Mary wiped at her eyes and then stooped to wipe the side of Sheila's chair and the puddle of urine on the floor beside it. "Stupid is as stupid does," she said softly.

Sheila looked at the young black woman with interest. "What's your name?"

"You want to know so you can report me?"

"Relax, I just want to know so I won't be saying 'Hey, girl-that-made-me-pee-myself, how's it going?'"

Mary looked at Sheila skeptically and then grinned a charming, bright smile. "Mary. Mary Johnson's my name. But my friends call me Queenie." She stuck out her hand, and Sheila shook it.

"I'm Sheila Taylor. But my friends call me Cripple." Mary looked shocked. "Ah, just kidding. Actually, my friends don't call nearly as much as they used to. They're all getting on with their lives, I guess."

"I'm sorry." Mary said, and her eyes strayed to the cards from the track team and the pictures from some of her races that were tacked on the wall above her bed.

"Did you go to Central High?" Sheila asked.

"No," Mary said quickly and went about emptying the remainder of the leg bag into the commode in Sheila's rest room.

"So where did you go to high school?"

"Nowhere. My dad got killed when some gang-bangers robbed the corner store while he was in it," Mary said matter-of-factly as she returned the leg bag to Sheila's chair. "My mom was sick, so I went to work. I left seventh grade and never went back."

Sheila pondered this a moment and could think of nothing to say in response. When Mary had finished her work, she turned to face Sheila. "I'm sorry again for the mess. If they don't fire me today, I'll try to do better to-morrow." And with that she left.

That night Sheila counted her pills again: twenty-nine. She tucked them under her mattress and closed her eyes. One more and she could kiss all of this good-bye.

"Good morning, Sheila! " Sunlight poured through the windows as Mary pulled back the drapes.

"I see they didn't fire you," Sheila moaned as she swung her lifeless legs off the bed.

"Not yet. The head nurse told me you're supposed to be going back to school in another six weeks."

"Yeah, right. What a thrill."

Mary stared again at the pictures of Sheila with her high-school friends. "I always thought that someday I'd go back. I used to imagine what it would feel like to walk up in front of everybody to get a diploma."

"So what's keeping you from doing it?" Sheila asked as Mary helped her into her wheelchair.

"I tried once. Never could pass the English test." She stooped to carefully loosen Sheila's leg bag and then emptied it in the rest room. "Can't read worth a lick. I couldn't take time to go back to school, and I just haven't got the brains to do it on my own."

Sheila rolled to the window and, stretching her arms, yawned loudly. "Sounds like you need to get yourself a tutor."

"Can't afford one. And who's got the time to do it for free."

Something in her voice touched Sheila deep within. After no more than a moment's thought, she said: "Say, Queenie. How would you like to graduate?"

With just five months till graduation, it wouldn't be easy, but something about Mary gave Sheila energy. Her pile of pills under the mattress was soon forgotten, and beginning that day, Sheila focused all her will power on helping Mary Johnson graduate from high school. She contacted her guidance counselor, got a copy of the English textbook, and began to tutor Mary.

When the supervisors at the rehab center learned of Sheila's project, they gave Mary extra time each day to work with her "tutor". The study sessions weren't always easy. "I'm too old for this," Mary said after getting back an essay covered with corrections from Sheila's red pen. "I'm nearly thirty-four."

"And I'm in a wheelchair! Get over it and rewrite that essay," Sheila shot back with a grin. They worked hard for six weeks, but when it came time for Sheila to leave the rehab, Mary was still not ready for the exam: She failed three practice tests and seemed ready to throw in the towel.

"Let's admit it," Mary said, "this is one race you just ain't going to win."

"Don't you count us out yet, girl," Sheila said. When she got her specially equipped van, Sheila had to start back to school as well. But three days a week after class, she would swing by the center and work with Mary.

With only two weeks to go till graduation, it was time for Mary to sit for the real test. "Just don't get pee on anybody, and you'll do great! " She had whispered to Mary as she entered the examination hall. That had been seventy-two agonizing hours ago. Mary was to get the results of the test that very afternoon, and they had agreed that if she passed, she would meet Sheila here, behind the gym, and walk behind her to receive her diploma.

Sheila peered at the crowd of seniors in caps and gowns gathering at the gym's rear door. Mary was nowhere to be seen. The band was beginning to play, and the other seniors were lining up. As Sheila rolled toward her place in line, she fought back tears. She knew that Mary might not pass. The exam was a tough one. She even thought about leaving the ceremony altogether, but her family was there to watch her roll across the platform, and she didn't want to disappoint them.

As the marching music began, Sheila started to roll her chair, but it wouldn't budge. She checked the brakes and then pushed again, but the chair stayed stuck. Then a hand tapped her on the shoulder. "You weren't thinking of going without me, were you?" Mary stood behind her, dressed in a cap and gown, holding the wheelchair and grinning that big smile.

"You made it! " Sheila cried. "Congrats, Queenie! "

"And congrats to you, girl," Mary said as she began to push Sheila's chair down the long aisle, "for making a good choice."

"What, to help you out?" Sheila asked as they rolled to the handicapped section in the front row of the graduating class.

"No. For deciding to quit collecting these." Mary dropped a small plastic bag in Sheila's lap and sat down in a folding chair beside her. Sheila picked up the bag. In it were twenty-nine pain pills. "Found them under your mattress that first morning before I woke you."

After a long moment Sheila said, "I guess you knew what I really needed."

"Somebody knew." Mary smiled. "Come on. Let's go get some diplomas."

And they did.

玛丽的毕业故事

希拉开着车，停在学校体育馆后面的残疾人停车场里，她的脸上露出了笑容。自从她坐上轮椅之后，停车实际上成了为数不多的更方便去做的事情之一。她把固定在篷车方向盘前面的轮椅解开，朝后转动到升降梯上，把自己往下放到人行道上。想着才3个月这一切便成了她的第二习性，她又一次笑了。

那是一个闷热的8月早晨，在哈里斯大街上，她的脚突然踩翻了边石，滑到了一辆丰田车的轮下。一群参加跨境长跑的姑娘们正在接受日常严格的夏季集训。像往常一样，希拉远远地跑在其他人

83

的前面。只有吉姆·米勒跟得很近,看到了事故的发生。"你看上去像一位天使……飞了起来。"她后来在医院里对希拉说道。

实际上她是真的飞了起来——根据交警的报告,她飞出了36英尺远。医生说这是个奇迹,她竟然活了下来。在前48小时里,她处于昏迷状态,她常去的教堂不停地为她祈祷。当她醒来后,他们又为她还能够跑步而祈祷。后来的祈祷没有灵验,因为希拉下后背的三根脊椎骨已经粉碎性骨折了。巨大的压力几乎截断了脊柱,她的下半身失去了知觉,不能自控。

3个月以来,她每天早晨醒来都祈祷这一切不过是一场噩梦。但是很快,她的祈祷改变了:"如果我再也不能走路了,上帝啊,让我死吧。"然而,即使这样的请求也没有得到满足:她的心脏状态良好,医生耐心地向她保证说她能够过上"正常的生活"……只是

坐在轮椅上。希拉决定自己满足自己的祈祷。她开始悄悄地收集止

痛片，这是康复中心值夜班的护士在她抱怨不能入睡时很不情愿

地给她的。希拉盘算着如果她能收集到30片，就一次性服下它们，

这样就能如愿了。30天，需要30天的时间。

在第28天，玛丽·约翰生把尿泼洒在希拉的膝盖上。

"你在干什么！"希拉叫了起来，眼瞅着湿热的黄色液体从她

的"尿囊"里溅了出来，浸湿了她白色的短裤。

"哦哦哦，对不起，小姐，我又弄得糟透了。"玛丽试图止住尿

液的流淌，可是她一拿起尿袋反而使得尿流得更多了。

"蠢货，放手，放手吧！"希拉用力拿开玛丽拿尿囊的手，然后

自己紧紧地捏住了导管的一端。"拿开它之前你得先松开皮带，然

后用夹子夹住，难道你不知道吗？"

"对不起，夫人，我应该等待贝尼斯特夫人来帮帮我的，请别吱声了，"玛丽的眼睛里充满了恳求。"我昨天刚上班，但是我是不准备能干出什么名堂的，我知道自己。"

"嘿，对一位姑娘来说，地板上的一点尿不是什么最坏的事情。"

玛丽擦了擦眼睛，然后蹲下身子擦拭着希拉的椅子边沿以及旁边地板上的一摊尿。"蠢人干蠢事。"她轻轻地说道。

希拉很感兴趣地打量起这位年轻的黑人妇女。"你叫什么名字？"

"您想知道我的名字来告我的状吗？"

"放心吧，我只是想知道，这样我就不会说'喂，尿我裤子上的那位姑娘，发生什么啦？'"

玛丽怀疑地看着希拉，然后露出了迷人而爽朗的微笑。"玛丽，玛丽·约翰生是我的名字。但是我的朋友们叫我奎尼。"她伸出了手，与希拉握了握。

"我叫希拉·泰勒，但是我的朋友们喊我瘸子。"玛丽看上去很吃惊。"啊,开开玩笑罢了。实际上,我的朋友们不像以前那样喊得多了,他们都在忙于自己的生活吧,我想。"

"对不起。"玛丽说道。她的眼光飘忽到她床头上的墙面上,那里用大头针钉着田径队的队卡以及她参赛的一些照片。

"您上过高中吗?"希拉问道。

"没有,"玛丽迅速地回答,一边把尿袋里剩下的尿倒进希拉房间厕所里的便桶里。

"那么你在哪儿上的高中?"

"哪儿也没有。我的父亲在一家街头小店里遇到一帮抢劫的歹徒,被杀死了,"玛丽如实地说道,一边把尿袋送回到希拉的椅子上。"我妈妈病了,所以我只好来工作。我只上到七年级就再没上下去了。"

希拉深思了一会儿,不知道怎样回答才好。玛丽干完活后,转身面对着希拉。"再次说抱歉,给您添麻烦了,如果他们今天不解雇我,我明天一定努力干得更好。"说完,离开了房间。

那天晚上,希拉又数了数她的药片:29片。她把药片塞到被褥下面,闭上了眼睛。再多一粒药,她就能和这一切说再见了。

"早上好,希拉!"玛丽拉起窗帘,阳光透过窗户照了进来。

"我看他们并没有解雇你啊,"希拉呻吟着,一边在床上拖动着那双无力的腿。

"还没呢,护士长告诉我再过6周你就能回到学校了。"

"啊,好的,太让人激动了。"

玛丽又一次紧盯着希拉同她高中朋友们的合影。"我总是想着将来某一天我要回去,我常常想象着在众人面前接过文凭是一种什么样的感觉。"

"那么是什么原因阻止你上高中的呢?"希拉问道,一边在玛丽的帮助下坐到轮椅上。

"我曾经试着考过,但是从来没能通过英语考试。"她弯下腰小心地解开希拉的尿袋,然后送到卫生间里倒掉。"不读书没用啊。我抽不出时间回到学校,而且也没有能力自学。"

希拉把轮椅推到窗前,伸开双臂响亮地打着哈欠。"听起来好像你需要请一位家庭教师。"

"没钱去请,谁有时间免费为别人辅导呀。"

她的声音里有一种东西深深地触动了希拉。思考片刻之后,她说道,"喂,奎尼,你很想毕业吗?"

离毕业只剩下5个月了,可不是一件容易的事情,然而玛丽的故事给了希拉力量。她很快就忘记了藏在被褥下面的一堆药,从那天开始,她集中所有的精力努力想帮助玛丽·约翰生从高中毕业。她联系上了她的导师,拿到了一本英语课本,开始辅导玛丽。

康复中心的管理者们获悉了希拉的计划后,每天为她安排了额外的时间让她和"导师"一起学习。学习的过程不总是一帆风顺的。"我太老了,学不好了,"当玛丽拿回一篇上面全是希拉用红笔修改了的论文时,她不禁说道。"我年近34了!"

"我可是坐在轮椅上啊!克服一下,把文章重写一遍,"希拉微笑着反驳道。她们辛勤工作了6周,可是当希拉出院的时候,玛丽仍然没有准备好考试:她3次模拟考试失败,显然打算放弃了。

"我们不得不承认,"玛丽说道,"这是一场你不会获胜的比赛。"

"难道你把我们也包括在内吗,姑娘,"希拉说道。当特制的篷车拿到后,希拉便不得不回到学校了。然而,一周3天,下课以后,她总是回到康复中心,和玛丽一起学习。

离毕业只剩2周了,玛丽参加正式考试的时候到了。"别把尿洒在别人身上啦,不许输给任何人,你会成功的!"在玛丽走进考试大厅前,希拉在她耳边轻声说道。难熬的72个小时过去了,那天

玛丽的毕业故事

下午，玛丽就要取得考试的结果了。她们曾经有过约定，如果她通过了，她将在体育馆的后面与希拉见面，然后推着她去接受毕业文凭。

一群穿着长袍戴着方帽的毕业生聚集在体育馆的后门，希拉怔怔地看着他们，可是没有看见玛丽。乐队开始奏乐了，其他的毕业生排起了队伍。希拉强忍着眼泪，转动着轮椅朝队伍走去。她想玛丽可能没有通过。这次考试题目很难。她甚至也想离开毕业典礼，然而她的家人在现场期待目视着她走过主席台，她不想让他们失望。

随着进行曲的响起，希拉开始转动她的轮椅，可是它动不起来。她检查了一下刹车，又接着推动，但是轮椅还是动不了。这时，一只手拍了拍她的肩膀。"你没有想着和我一起去，是吗?"玛丽身着长袍，头戴方帽站在她身后，手抓着轮椅，脸上露出了开心的微笑。

"你通过了！"希拉喊了起来。"恭喜啊，奎尼！"

"也恭喜你，小姐，"玛丽边说边开始推动轮椅，顺着长长的过道走过去，"恭喜你做出了正确的选择。"

"什么选择，帮助了你吗？"希拉问道。这时她们来到了位于毕业班前排的残疾人专座上。

"不是，恭喜你决定放弃收集这些东西。"玛丽把一个小塑料袋扔到希拉的腿上，然后在她旁边的一张折叠椅上坐下。希拉拿起袋子，看见里面有29粒止痛药。"这是第一天早晨在喊醒你之前，我在你的被褥下面发现的。"

经过了一段长时间的沉默后，希拉说道，"我猜你知道我真正需要什么了。"

"有人知道。"玛丽笑了。"快点，让我们拿毕业文凭去吧。"

她们走上前去。

Chapter 4

Balancing Priorities

4

人生的天平

Above all,
carefully guard your heart,
for it is the wellspring
of your life!
As you grow in wisdom
and apply your heart
to understanding,
you'll learn what is right, just, and fair
and how to make good choices.
Discretion will protect you, and
understanding will guard you.
When you delight in me,
I'll give you the things
your heart truly desires.

BLESSINGS,
YOUR GOD OF LOVE

—from Proverbs 4:23; 2:2–11; Psalm 37:4

首先，
小心呵护你的心脏，
因为那是你的生命之源！
随着你智慧的增长，
学会了用心思考，
你会懂得什么是
正确、正义和公平，
并且知道如何做出正确的选择。
谨慎会为你撑开保护伞，
理解也会成为
你的避风港湾。
如果你因为我感到喜悦，
我将给予你心仪的一切。

诚挚祝福，
你的爱神

——摘自：《箴言》4：23；2：2-11；《诗篇》37：4

It has been said that the future is like a walk on a windy day. You can hide from each gust, drawing your coat ever closer around you, or you can take joy in the way the wind makes the trees sway and the leaves dance.

Carefulness or caring: Which is more important?

They are the twin oars that move us safely but passionately through life. They are the compass points that keep us on course. Living a life that is careful and yet fully committed to care for others is a delicate balance. Dangers are real, and more than one pilgrim has been blown off course because he or she threw caution to the wind and ignored a coming storm.

Loving will always be risky business. So guard your heart as precious and holy, but offer it fully to the friends who grace your life.

Lord, let me be careful but full of care. Guide me that I may live fully and love wisely.

有人曾经说过,未来就像是在起风的日子里

的一场散步。你可以裹紧大衣,躲避阵风,也可以欣赏

风吹树动、树叶飞舞的美景。

小心或关心:哪一个更重要?

在生活的河流中,它们是一对船桨,平稳而猛

烈地推动着我们向前。它们又是指南针,让我

们保持着正确的航向。过一种小心谨

慎而又全心全意关心他人的

生活是一种微妙的

平衡。危

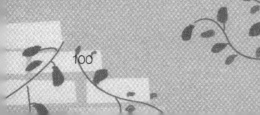

险真实地存在着，众多的朝圣者被吹离了

航线，因为他或她没有步步留神，而且忽略了暴风雨的

到来。

爱总是会有风险的，所以，保护好你那颗珍贵的、圣

洁的心吧。但是，面对给你生活增添了光彩的朋友，

请敞开你的胸怀吧。

上帝啊，请让我小心谨慎而又充满

爱心吧，引导我过一种美满而

又不乏睿智的爱的

生活吧。

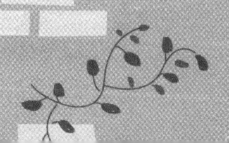

Love is a beautiful flower that blossoms on earth, with its roots embedded in eternity.

—Marvea Johnson

爱是一朵美丽的花，它绽放在人世间，根植于永恒之中。

——马韦尔·约翰逊

"You are on the
dog level of Cantonese,"
Grandma Rose had explained one day.
"you know what is
spoken to you,
but you cannot
answer back!"

"你的粤语水平很蹩脚，"
有一天祖母曾挑明道，
"你听得懂我说的话，
但是却不能回答我！"

"You are on the
dog level of Cantonese,'
Grandma Rose had explained one day.
"You know what is
spoken to you,
but you cannot
answer back!"

Small Heart, Close Heart

"Over the river and through the woods to Grand-mother's house we go..." The line from the old song had gotten stuck in an endless loop in Soo Lin's head again. She smiled to herself as the Golden Gate Bridge came into view: The writers of that song had never met her Grandma Rose. As she pulled her car into the toll lane, the lyrics she had devised for that song as a child came back: "Over the Bay Bridge through Chinatown to Grand-mother's house we go..."

Soo Lin's mother began to scramble for her purse to get the change for the toll. "Mom, you don't need to do that anymore." Soo Lin said, tapping the little transmitting device that automatically deducted money from their account each time they drove through one of the growing number of toll booths on the California freeways,

"I keep forgetting. Technology! What will they come up with next?" Her mother shut her purse and flipped down the visor to check her makeup. She always got a little tense when they were heading to Grandma Rose's place. Soon the hilly streets of Chinatown were all around them. They passed shops that looked as if they had been there since the Gold Rush had turned San Francisco from a dirt-poor outpost to a shining "city on the hill". Merchants with signs in Chinese offered spices and ancient herbal remedies. But this was Grandma Rose's corner of the world. Technology was making no inroads here, She had laughed out loud when her granddaughter had tried to talk her into a computer.

"Foolishness! " she had muttered in her native Cantonese.   "Should I take my brain out and put it on a shelf? I can make my own decisions without the help of a box of wires."

"But Grandma Rose, if you had a computer, I could e-mail you," Soo Lin had argued.

"What? To tell me you don't have time to come visit? I want to see your face—not a TV screen."

Soo Lin had considered mentioning the new video phone technology,   but she knew at heart that her grandmother was right.   Every technological advance brought new ways to communicate without touching one another.   The digital revolution was substituting bytes for hugs and e-mails for visits.   But Grandma Rose was a fearless warrior in the battle for human contact.   When Soo Lin had gotten so busy during her sophomore year in high school that she had not called or seen her grandmother for several weeks, Grandma Rose had sent her a letter—make that a summons—on beautiful scented stationery:

My dear Soo Lin,

Are you dead?   If not,   please prove this by coming to my house for Kung Po chicken this weekend.

Yours truly,

Grandma Rose

You never had to ask Grandma Rose twice what she was thinking. "What happened to all that Asian reserve and shyness that Chinese women are supposed to have?" Soo Lin teased her one afternoon.

"Sorry. I was gone the day that was passed out," Grandma Rose had said with a wink.

Soo Lin turned onto Lake Street and parked in front of #333. Her grandmother's small yard was ablaze in flowers. It looked like a rainbow had crash-landed in her garden. Her green thumb was notorious in her neighborhood, and Grandma Rose kept her friend's tables supplied with bouquets of the most gorgeous blossoms all year long. "That's what I love about San Francisco weather," Grandma Rose often said. "You can pick a fresh flower any day of the year."

Soo Lin pulled carefully to the curb and set the parking brake on the steep hill as her mother took one last look in the mirror. Soo Lin glanced in her mirror as well. Her dark eyes and jet-black hair were about the only things that would have identified her as being partly Asian, though technically she was Eurasian. ("Like Tiger Woods? Cool." one classmate had said with admiration.) Grandma Rose, on the other hand, was 100-percent Chinese. She had met and married Soo Lin's grandfather during World War Ⅱ, and after the fighting was over, he brought his new bride to his home state. Since 1946, she had lived, worked, and raised three daughters in San Francisco. Soo Lin's mother, the youngest of the three girls, looked the least Asian of the group, but Soo Lin had tapped into some of those recessive genes and was a striking mix of East and West. She locked and alarmed the car and walked arm in arm with her mother up the steps to Grandma Rose's front door.

Grandma Rose had sent her most recent "summons" letter three weeks ago. Her age and her health were not cooperating, and so attending soo Lin's graduation ceremony down in the valley was just out of the question. The combination of the long ride and the hot sun was more than she could handle. But Grandma wanted to have her moment with the graduate before the big day. "Bring your mother and try to be here by noon." Soo Lin rang the bell and glanced at her watch: it was 11:58—Grandma Rose would be impressed.

"You're early! " a shrill voice called as she began to unlock the series of deadbolts that protected her from the ever-changing outside world.

"Hello, Momma," Soo Lin's mother said in Cantonese when the big door finally swung open. She hugged Rose's neck and stepped aside so she could greet Soo Lin.

"Hi, Grandma Rose! You look great," Soo Lin said without needing to exaggerate: Grandma Rose did look great. She was wearing a floral print dress that looked as if it could have been plucked straight from her front yard. Her jet-black hair was pulled back into a tight bun, and her eyes gleamed like little black pearls.

"I had to get dressed up for the big graduate. Don't want you to be embarrassed at Loo Fong's." Grandma had made reservations at her favorite Chinese restaurant. Reservations weren't actually needed, but she had called Pat Fong and asked her to prepare Cantonese duck for this special lunch. "Let's get going. If they overcook the duck, we may as well eat Kentucky Fried Chicken?"

The lunch was delightful. Grandma Rose was in rare form—telling stories, partly in Cantonese and partly in English, about her childhood in China and her school years in Singapore. Soo Lin couldn't speak much of her grandmother's native tongue, but she could understand almost every word. ("You are at the dog level of Cantonese," Grandma Rose had explained one day. "You know what is spoken to you, but you cannot answer back! ")

The duck was indeed delicious, and as the lunch drew to a close, Mrs. Fong brought a plate of fortune cookies to the table. Grandma Rose took the tray and offered one to her daughter, took one for herself, and extended the last one to Soo Lin. As she lifted it from the tray, it felt heavier than expected, and when she cracked it open, she knew why. A beautiful cloisonne heart had somehow been tucked inside it,   along with the normal fortune strip. Soo Lin looked up at her grandmother, who was smiling a mischievous smile. "Now that's what I call a fortune," she said.

Soo Lin read the little slip of paper that had been wrapped around the heart. It was not the typical printed type,   but rather it was handwritten in her grandmother's unmistakable printing. It read, "Small heart, Close heart."

Soo Lin looked with confusion at her grandmother. "I was going to write it in Chinese,   but I knew you couldn't read it," Grandma Rose said with a grin.

Soo Lin spoke the words out loud: "Small heart, close heart." Then it hit her: In Chinese, word characters are combined to express other ideas. *Small heart* were the two Chinese words that together meant "be careful". *Close heart* on the other hand meant   "to care for someone".

"Be careful and care?"   Soo Lin asked in broken but

understandable Cantonese.

"Very good." Rose patted her daughter's hand. "At least *your* daughter will teach her children some Cantonese."

"Oh Momma, you know I tried." Soo Lin's mother said. Though none of her daughters had much of an ear for the intricacies of the spoken Chinese, Soo Lin was the best of the three.

"But what does it mean, Grandma Rose?" Soo Lin asked.

Rose took off her glasses and laid them beside her plate. "That heart was a gift from my grandmother when my family moved to Singapore. She was too frail and too set in her ways to come with us. But she wanted me to always remember China. Her brother was a craftsman— he made that heart himself. When she gave it to me, she asked me to do two things in my new home: Be careful but be full of care. *Small heart, close heart.*" Rose said these last words in Cantonese. As she said the words, she tightened her right hand into a fist while placing her left hand, fully opened, on her heart. "It means be careful of things and people that may hurt you, but never stop caring. These are the two most important things you must do...as you go on to college with all your computers and e-mails."

Soo Lin turned the beautiful heart over in her hand. On the back were the four Chinese characters for the words: *Small heart, Close heart.* She looked with love at her grandmother, who was letting a rare public tear escape her eye, and she repeated the Chinese words and then the English.

"'Be careful but full of care.' I will, Grandma Rose. I promise." Soo Lin squeezed the little heart pendant tightly in her right hand and reached out with her left to embrace her grandmother with tears of her own.

特殊的毕业礼物

"跨过小河，穿过森林，我们朝外婆的家中走去……"古老的歌词在苏·林的脑海里不停地萦绕着。当金门桥映入眼帘时，她暗自发笑起来：那首歌曲的创作者可是从来没有见过她的祖母罗斯呀。当她的车驶进收费车道时，她唱起了儿时改编的歌谣："跨过海湾桥，穿过唐人街，我们朝外婆的家中走去……"

苏·林的母亲慌忙拿过钱包，开始找零钱付过桥费。"妈妈，再也不必那么做了。"苏·林说完按了一下小小的传输器，这是她们

人 生 的 天 平

每次通过加州高速公路上不断增多的收费站时一种从账户上自动扣款的装置。

"我总是忘了,技术!接下来他们会发明什么呢?"她的妈妈收起钱包,一边拉下帽舌给自己补妆。每当她们去祖母罗斯的家中时,她总是有一点儿紧张。很快她们便置身于唐人街高楼耸立的街中。她们经过的那些街道好像自从淘金热把旧金山从破旧的边哨变成闪亮的"山城"时就已经存在了。一些打着汉语标记的商店出售着香料和远古中草药。但这是祖母罗斯的世界角落,技术还没有侵袭这里。外孙女曾经努力地说服祖母使用电脑,但是她哈哈大笑。

"愚蠢!"她用粤语方言喃喃自语。"难道我应该把脑子取出来放在书架上不成?用不了一盒子电线的帮忙,我就能自己做出决定。"

"但是罗斯祖母，如果你拥有一台电脑，我就能给你发电子邮件，"苏·林曾经争辩道。

"什么？你是说你没有时间来看望我？我想看的是你的脸——不是电脑屏幕。"

苏·林曾想提及新的视频电话技术，但是她心里明白祖母的话是对的。每一次技术的发展带给人们的都是新的不用彼此接触的交流方式，数字革命正在用字节替换着拥抱，用电子邮件代替了访问。但是在为了促进人类彼此交流的战役中，罗斯祖母是一位无畏的战士。在苏·林上高中二年级的时候，她因为很忙而一连几周没有去看望祖母或者给她打电话，于是罗斯祖母给她写了一封信——写成了一张告示——写在美丽芳香的信笺上：

我亲爱的苏·林：

你还活着吗？如果是，请于本周末来我的家中吃宫保鸡丁，以证明此事。

人　生　的　天　平

对于祖母想做的事情你从来不必询问第二次。"中国妇女应该持有的亚洲人的矜持和腼腆都跑到哪儿去了？"苏·林在一天下午打趣地问道。

"对不起，她们生出来的那天我刚好不在家，"祖母眨了一下眼睛说道。

苏·林驶上莱克大街，停在333号房前。祖母家的小院子里百花争艳，好像天上的彩虹散落了下来似的。她的养花技术在街坊邻居当中可是赫赫有名的，所以祖母朋友家的桌子上常年摆放着一束束祖母赠送的最娇艳的花朵。"这就是我喜欢旧金山天气的原因，"祖母常常说道，"你在一年当中的任何一天都能摘到鲜花。"

苏·林小心地把车开到路边，踩下刹车停在陡峭的山路上。她的妈妈最后一眼照了照镜子。苏·林也朝镜子里瞟了一眼自己，唯独她那深色的眼睛和乌黑的头发体现出她是亚裔人，虽然用专门术语说她是欧亚混血儿。（"像泰戈·伍兹？真酷！"一位同学曾经仰慕地说道。）另一方面，罗斯祖母则是100%的中国人。在二战期间，她与苏·林的祖父相识并结了婚。战争结束后，祖父带着他的新娘回到了自己的故乡。自从1946年以来，她便在旧金山生活、工作并养育了3个女儿。苏·林的妈妈是3个女儿中最小的一位，也是长得最不像亚洲人的一位，但是苏·林却继承了一些隐性基因特征，是一个典型的东西方混血儿。她锁好车，打开防盗报警器，然后挽着母亲的手走上罗斯祖母家门前的台阶。

罗斯祖母是在3周前发出她最近的一张"告示"信的。年龄和健康都由不得她了，所以下到山谷参加苏·林的毕业典礼只能是一种奢望，她哪能经受得起炎热的阳光和长途的颠簸呢？然而祖母却想在这一重大日子到来之前见一见这位毕业生。"同你的母亲一道,尽量在中午前赶到。"苏·林按响了门铃,又看了一下表:11点58分——祖母会被感动的。

"你们来得真早!"她尖声叫道,一边开始打开一道道将她与不断变化的外部世界相隔离的门闩。

"您好,妈妈,"大门打开时,苏·林的母亲用广东话说道。她拥抱过祖母,然后走到一边让她迎接苏·林。

"您好,祖母!您看上去真精神。"苏·林说得没有夸张:罗斯祖母看上去真的很精神。她穿着印花的衣服,仿佛刚刚从前院里摘来印在身上似的。她乌黑的头发被盘成了一个发髻,闪亮的眼睛像两颗黑珍珠。

"为了这位大毕业生,我得打扮打扮,不能让你们在罗凤餐馆里感到难为情啊。"祖母已经在她最喜欢的中餐馆预订了午餐。虽

然实际上并不需要订餐,但是她还是提前给潘凤打了电话,让她为

这顿特别的午餐准备一只广东烤鸭。"我们出发吧,如果他们把鸭

子烧煳了,我们也可以吃肯德基!"

午餐吃得很愉快。祖母表现出了少有的高兴劲儿——用夹杂

着粤语的英语讲述起她在中国的童年时代和在新加坡读书岁月的

故事。祖母的母语苏·林只能说一点儿,但是她能听懂几乎每一个

词。("你的粤语水平很蹩脚,"有一天祖母曾挑明道,"你听得懂

我说的话,但是却不能回答我!")

鸭子的确味美可口。午餐结束时,凤夫人又端上一盘子福饼。

祖母拿起盘子,递给女儿一块,自己留了一块,然后把最后一块传

给了苏·林。当苏·林从盘子里夹起饼时,她感觉这块饼比自己想象

中的要沉些,当她打开它时,她明白了为什么。一个美丽的心型景泰蓝不知什么时候被塞在里面,还有一张常见的运气纸条。苏·林抬头看着祖母, 只见她脸上露出了诡秘的微笑。"我说这就是命嘛,"她说。

苏·林拿起那张包裹着景泰蓝的小纸条念了起来。这不是那种典型的打印出来的纸条, 而是真真切切祖母手写的笔迹。上面写着, "Small heart, Close heart."

苏·林迷惑地看着祖母。"我准备用汉语写,但是我知道你不会念汉语,"祖母微微一笑。

苏·林大声念了出来:"Small heart, Close heart." 然后她悟了出来:在汉语里,汉字被组合在一起来表达其他的意思。Small heart是两个汉字,在一起的意思是"小心谨慎",Close heart 则表示"关心别人"。

"小心并关心?" 苏·林用很不流利但是能听得懂的粤语问道。

"太棒了。"罗斯拍着她女儿的手。"至少你的女儿将来能教她的孩子们一点粤语了。"

"噢妈妈,你知道,我努力学过。"苏·林的妈妈说道。虽然她的3个女儿都没有听过复杂的汉语口语,然而苏·林却是姐妹3个中学得最好的一个。

"可是这有什么含义啊,祖母?"苏·林问道。

罗斯把眼镜摘了下来,放在盘子旁边。"那颗心是我们搬到新加坡时我的祖母送给我的,她因为太脆弱,而且思想上固步自封,因而没有和我们一道搬迁,但是她希望我永远记住中国。她的兄弟是一位工匠——他亲手制作了那颗心。当她把它递给我时,她要求我到了新家时要做两件事情:小心谨慎但是充满爱心,小心,关心。"罗斯用粤语说出最后两个词。当她说这些话时,她的右手紧握成拳头,同时左手完全张开,放在自己的心上。"这意味着防人之心不可无,但是永远不要忘了关心他人。这是你必须做的两件最重要的事情……即使当你上了大学成天与电脑和电子邮件打交道时也不能忘记。"

　　苏·林在手里翻看着那颗美丽的心,看到它的背面印着四个汉字:小心,关心。她满怀深情地看着祖母,在众人面前落下了一颗泪珠,接着她用汉语和英语反复地念着那几个字。

　　"小心谨慎但是充满爱心。我会做到的,祖母,我保证。"苏·林用右手紧紧地攥着那个小小的心形坠饰,一边伸出左手拥抱着祖母,泪水流了出来。

Chapter 5

Choosing to Smile

⑤

微笑着面对

Always aim for kindness,
even when you've been wronged.
Being wronged doesn't justify
a wrong response.
The key is
letting your love abound
more and more in
knowledge and
depth of insight,
So that you may be able
to discern what is best
and may be pure and blameless
until the day of christ Jesus.

LOVE ALWAYS,
YOUR GOD OF FORGIVENESS

—from 1 Thessalonians 5:15; Philippians 1:9–10

即使当你受到了委屈，
也总是心怀仁慈，
因为以怨报怨是不对的。
关键是要让你的爱
更多地汇入到你的知识
和深邃的思想中，
于是你便能够分辨出
最美好的事情，
并且变得纯洁无瑕，
直到永远。

永远爱你的，
宽恕之神。

——摘自：《帖撒罗尼迦书》5：15；《腓力比书》1:9-10

It has been said that truly great people are those who have learned not only to be responsible but to be "response-able." The former is the quality of faithfulness in your assigned duties. The latter is the ability to choose how you will respond to life's challenges. Disappointments and mistreatment are impossible to avoid. But the spirit with which we respond makes all the difference in how those experiences bless or bruise us.

Living the life of

a doormat, accepting disrespect and scorn as normal, is not a virtue to be sought, but revenge and defensiveness can be just as damaging to our souls. Look for the path that handles libel with a laugh and responds to scorn with a smile. When we find the humor in the bleakest moments, we have also found the secret to enduring them.

God, help me smile at my enemies and disarm their hatred with humor.

有人曾说,那些不仅承担责任,而且"承担得起

责任"的人才是真正伟大的人。前者是一种忠于职守的

品质,后者则是面对生活的挑战如何应对的能力。失望和

虐待是不可避免的,但是,在祈佑或损害我们生活的

经历中,起决定作用的是我们勇于应对一切

的精神。

过着一种忍辱负重的生

活,平常的接受不敬与嘲讽并不是一种美德,然而,复仇与抵抗又只能挫伤我们的灵魂。寻找一种用欢笑代替诽谤,用微笑应对嘲讽的方法吧。当我们能够在最悲伤的时刻发现幽默,我们也就找到了忍受悲伤的秘诀。

上帝啊,帮帮我,让我以微笑面对敌人,用幽默消除他们的仇恨吧。

There is wonderful freedom
and joy in coming to recognize
that the fun is in the becoming.
—Gloria Gaither

意识到欢乐即将来临也就意味着体会到了美妙的自由和愉悦。

——格洛里亚·盖瑟

如果这会儿他弄砸了，
他甚至有可能
　　　被逐出毕业典礼大会。

If he messed up now,
he might even get
kicked out
of the assembly.

A Moment to Remember

It really had been Jack's idea from the start.

Eric repeated this to himself again and again as the little lump in his shirt pocket moved once more. It was a-mazing that no one had noticed it. He had made it all the way to the rows of seats in the front of the field house that were reserved for the graduating class. From here he had a clear view of the whole gym. It had been decorated in red and blue crepe-paper flowers—the work of the Junior League Girls. Eric's sister would be part of that select group next year. But tonight she and his parents were sitting high up in the bleachers. His dad would have the binoculars, and his mom would be clutching her package of tissues. If his mother had known what resided in his pocket today, she would have needed more than tissues. But if the plan went well, she'd never have to know.

The whole thing had been concocted over a Grande Burrito special at Manny's Cantina three weeks before graduation. Jack Freeman, Steve Santa Ana, and Todd Perkins had all gathered for their regular Friday Mexican lunch.

"It's just not fair! " Jack mumbled as he stabbed at his burrito with a vengeance.

"What's not fair?" Eric asked. The last to arrive, he waved to Manny behind the counter as he took his seat next to Jack.

"Life! " Steve shot back as Todd nodded vigorously. "Life...and Liz Slater." The very mention of that name brought another grunt from Jack and a final vicious jab into his battered burrito. Liz Slater was the editor of the school newspaper and head of the student graduation committee. And it was she who had devised the brilliant idea of picking the student to give the graduation address by "blind essay submission". The theme was "A Moment to Remember", and any student who wanted could submit an essay for the committee to review. The names would be left off the review copies so that, as Liz said, "the best person would be chosen devoid of the politics that often taint such decisions."

The plan had not produced the results Liz had hoped for. When the votes were counted, the winning essay belonged to none other than Jack Freeman—the opinion-page editor for the school's paper and Liz Slater's least favorite person. Nearly every one of Jack's highly amusing articles had managed to offend Liz or one of her friends at some point during his two-year stint in that job. Liz had tried to get him booted off the editorial staff so many times it was a running joke at each meeting. "So what are you going to try to get me fired for this week, Lizzy?" Jack would croon.

When it was revealed that Jack had been chosen to give the graduation speech, you would have thought Pee Wee Herman had been elected "Man of the Century". Half of the student body was appalled, while the other half just shook their heads and grinned in anticipation of what would surely be the most entertaining speech in the school's history.

And Elizabeth Slater was livid. "Jack Freeman, if you embarrass me or this school..." She had ranted one day.

"Lizzy! Put your ax away, sweetie. I promise I won't embarrass you." And Eric knew Jack meant it. Jack secretly admired Liz's talents and had even asked her out once, but the socialite would never give him the time of day.

"So what's up with Liz Slater?" Eric asked as Manny brought him his regular Grande special.

"She got Jack kicked off the graduation program," Todd said.

"No way! "

"Not only that," Steve added through a mouthful of burrito. "She went behind his back to Mr. Bryan and told him Jack was going to embarrass the whole administration with some prank."

"And," Todd chimed in, "she's gonna pass it off as Jack's idea. Like he wanted her to speak in his place."

"You've got to be joking," Eric exclaimed.

"She's won this one, guys," Jack said softly. "And there's nothing I can do about it."

"Why don't you just expose her, Jack? Write an

article and let her have it."

"And what would that get me? A few more enemies."

"But, Jack, we gotta do something," Steve and Todd said nearly in stereo.

"Well, I did have one idea...but I would need some help."

"All right, let's hear it," Eric said, pushing the remains of his burrito aside.

"I heard from Karen Peters that Liz has had her speech planned for some time. She's gonna bring this paper bag, and at the big moment in her speech, she's gonna reach in and pull out her baby shoes to make a sentimental point about all the steps of our lives."

"So?" asked Eric.

"I just thought we might give her a little surprise when she reaches in the bag."

Big silly grins began to spread across the conspirators' faces.

"The only problem is I don't sit near her at the assembly. However, I managed to get a peek at the seating chart, and guess who sits right behind little Miss Speech

Stealer?" Jack slowly turned to stare at Eric....

"All rise for the pledge of allegiance," Mr. Bryan said with a wave of his hands. Eric stood carefully and placed his hand over his heart. This was it. He felt the little lump shift as he touched his robe and knew this wasn't going to be as easy as Jack had made it seem that day over burritos. He shot a quick glance at Jack three rows away. Jack just nodded and said with his eyes, "You can do it, man! "

Standing directly in front of Eric, clutching her big speech in her left hand, was Liz Slater. And sitting under her chair was the infamous little brown bag. This was the moment Eric had been running through in his mind all day. If he messed up now, he might even get kicked out of the assembly. But just as his courage was wavering, Liz Slater turned and shot a smug smile at Jack Freeman, who just smiled back and winked. "Jack the Jerk," she muttered loud enough for others to hear.

OK, Liz, Eric thought, It's *time for justice.* As the pledge began, he reached up to find the end of his tassel and gave it a little tug. His cap tumbled to the ground, and as he bent down to retrieve it, he made certain no one was watching him. He shot his hand into his pocket and retrieved Clarence, his sister's pet frog, and dropped him into the bag with Liz's baby shoes. Eric stood back up just as the pledge was winding down and tried to keep from smiling too broadly as he joined the rest: "and justice for all."

The next few minutes seemed to move in slow motion. The student band did their normal, slightly-out-of-tune version of the school anthem. Mr. Bryan made a few dry comments, and then it was time. Liz Slater rose and headed for the stage, carrying her little paper bag. As she passed Jack's row, she gave him one more triumphant grin and mounted the stage.

"As most of you know, Jack Freeman was originally chosen to give this address, but he felt that what I have to say was what you needed to hear, and I thank him for that." Jack just smiled, and there was scattered applause. Jack glanced back at Eric, who gave him the prearranged thumbs-up sign.

"I stand before you today," Liz went on,   "with a treasure beside me." She gestured to the paper bag, and as she did, it moved ever so slightly. Eric thought he would choke, but Liz didn't seem to notice, "What I am about to show you represents the steps that you and I have made and will make as we move toward our future. Do any of you remember these..."

Then she did it: Liz Slater reached into her little brown bag and pulled out a pair of baby shoes...with a fully grown toad sitting in one of them. Clarence, the toad, let out a perfectly timed croak and leaped onto the podium. Liz stood frozen, staring at the green creature. And then she made her biggest mistake of the evening: She screamed. Clarence, who doesn't take well to loud noises, leaped from the podium and onto Liz's graduation gown, disappearing under her collar. Liz panicked, began flailing at the zipper of her gown, backed into the band director's music stand, and fell into the first-chair flute player's lap. It was at that moment that Clarence, who must have been just as frightened as Liz, managed to hop out of her gown and land squarely on the second-chair flutist's lap. At this, the whole flute section broke into pandemonium, and in the crash of folding chairs and falling music stands, Liz Slater managed to crawl right into the bass drum stand, which collapsed on her unceremoniously.

Mr. Bryan was still trying to determine what had happened when Jack made it to the podium. His timing was nothing short of perfect.

"Thanks, Liz," Jack said loudly into the microphone, "for helping with that little stunt. Relax, folks, we've had this planned for some time. I think we fooled them all, Liz! "

Mr. Bryan stared at Jack and then turned to look at Liz, who was still trying to extricate herself from the bass drum stand with the tuba player's help. The senior class began to laugh, and when Steve and Todd started applauding, it swept across the whole audience.

One of the trumpet players had managed to catch Clarence, and he walked up and handed the toad over to Jack. Liz, who was finally back on her feet and trying to figure out what had happened, saw everyone applauding and did the only think she could think to do: She bowed.

"Wasn't she convincing, folks? Come here, Liz." Jack called. And the applause grew louder. As she reached the podium, Jack put his arm around her and whispered, "Stick with me, and you'll get out of this OK." Then he turned to the audience and said seriously,   "This Little lady and I just wanted you all to know that life is not just a series of baby steps, for many occasions require us to take great leaps! Right, Liz?" Liz nodded vigorously, praying it was the right choice.   "And beginning today, you and I are taking one of the biggest leaps. We are leaping into the future..."

And with that Jack Freeman began the speech of a lifetime. The student body stopped him five times with thunderous applause. When he finished, he shook Liz's hand, and they both took one more bow before marching back toward their seats to a standing ovation. As he was helping her down the steps, Liz leaned close to Jack and whispered, "Why did you do that? You could have made a fool of me."

Jack grinned his trademark grin and said, "Oh no, I was just looking for a way for both of us to leave here with a moment to remember." And with that, he hugged her and headed for his seat, pondering whether Liz Slater might want a Coke after the graduation assembly.

毕业典礼的难忘时刻

其实从一开始就是杰克的主意。

艾瑞克的心里一直嘀咕着，感觉到衬衫口袋里的那一团小东西又动了一下。很奇怪，没有人注意到它。他一直把它装在身上，直到来到为毕业班留设的更衣室前面的座位上。从这儿他能很清楚地看见整个体育馆。馆内已经被红蓝色的绉纸装扮得耀眼夺目——这是青年女子联盟会姑娘们的杰作。明年艾瑞克的妹妹将会成为这一卓越组织的成员。然而今天晚上他的妹妹和他的父母正坐在高高的露天看台上。他的爸爸准会拿着望远镜观看，而他的妈妈则会攥着一大把的纸巾等着擦眼泪了，如果今天他的妈妈已

经知道了他的口袋里装着什么东西的话,她会需要更多的纸巾。但是如果计划进行顺利的话,她将永不得知。

整个事件的策划还得从毕业3周前在拉米小酒吧的一次玉米饼大聚餐上谈起。杰克·弗里曼、斯蒂夫·桑特阿娜和托德·普肯斯照例举行他们的星期五墨西哥午餐。

"就是不公平!"杰克一边咀嚼,一边愤愤地戳向他的玉米饼。

"什么不公平?"艾瑞克问道。他最后一个到达,一边朝柜台后面的拉米挥了挥手,一边在杰克旁边的座位上坐了下来。

"生活!"斯蒂夫冒了一句,托德狠劲地点着头。"生活……还有莉斯·斯莱特。"一提到这个名字,杰克又咕噜了一声,并且对他那块被戳得稀巴烂了的玉米饼发出了最后的恶毒一击。莉斯·斯莱特是校报的编辑以及学生毕业委员会的主任。正是她想出了通过"无记名论文送审"的方式来选拔学生做毕业发言的好主意的,发言的主题是"难忘的时刻"。任何想发言的同学都可以提交一篇论文经委员会审阅，论文撰写人的姓名将会从审阅稿中被画掉，这样，正如莉斯所言，"将会避免常常玷污此事的政治因素而选出最佳的人选。"

计划并没有产生出莉斯所希望的结果。数完选票后，获胜的论文不属于别人而正是杰克·弗里曼——校报的意见栏编辑，莉斯·斯莱特的论文得票最少。在杰克从事编辑工作的两年里，他的几乎每一篇超级搞笑的文章都曾经在某些方面冒犯了莉斯或者她的一位朋友。有许多次，莉斯曾试图将他逐出编辑队伍，但是每一次都成了人们的笑谈。"莉斯，本周你准备用什么办法解聘我呀？"杰克常常低声问道。

当结果揭晓，杰克当选为毕业生发言代表时，你会想到曾经当选为"世纪人物"的皮·韦·荷曼。学生中有一半人感到震惊，另一半人则摇摇头，笑嘻嘻地期盼着学校历史上最有趣的演讲到来。

伊丽莎白·斯莱特脸色铁青。有一天她嚷叫道，"杰克·弗里曼，如果你让我或者学校难堪的话……"

"莉斯！收起你那套吧，亲爱的，我保证不会让你难堪。"艾瑞克知道杰克说到做到。杰克暗下里很佩服莉斯的才能，而且曾经邀请她一起外出，可是这位社会活动积极分子从来没有给过他一次机会。

"那么莉斯·斯莱特怎么样啦？"艾瑞克问道。这时，拉米为他端上了特制的大玉米饼。

"她把杰克踢出了毕业发言，"托德说道。

"真没办法！"

"不仅如此，"斯蒂夫嘴里含着饼补充道，"她私下里见到布莱恩先生，告诉他杰克想开玩笑让整个行政班子感到难堪。"

"而且，"托德附和道，"她准备欺骗说这是杰克的注意，是杰克让她代替他发言的。"

"你真是在开玩笑，"艾瑞克大声嚷道。

"这一次她赢了，伙伴们，"杰克轻声地说道。"对此我无能为力了。"

"为什么不揭露她，杰克？写一篇文章，让她受受。"

"那对我有什么好处？只会招致更多的敌人。"

"不过,杰克,我们得做点什么。"斯蒂夫和托德几乎是异口同声地说道。

"啊,我倒是有一个主意……但是我需要一些帮助。"

"没问题,让我们听听,"艾瑞克说着把剩下的饼推到了一边。

"我从凯伦·彼得斯那儿听说,莉斯的发言稿已经准备好有一段时间了。她准备提着这种纸袋,在演讲的关键时刻,伸手从纸袋里拿出她的娃娃鞋声情并茂地描述我们生命的所有历程。"

"那么会怎样？"艾瑞克问道。

"我只是想在她的手伸进纸袋时,我们或许可以给她一点儿小小的惊讶。"

串谋者们的脸上一个个开始露出了开心的、傻傻的微笑。

"唯一的问题就是,在毕业典礼大会上我不坐在她的旁边。不过,我已经瞥见了座位表,你们猜猜谁正好坐在这位窃人发言权小姐的身后呢?"杰克慢慢地转过头,盯着艾瑞克……

"全体起立,举行宣誓仪式,"布莱恩先生挥动着双手说。艾瑞克小心站起来,用手捂着心窝。是时候了。当他的手触摸到礼袍时,他感觉到那一团小东西在移动。他明白,一切将不会像杰克那天在面饼聚会上所说的那样轻松。他瞅了一眼离他有三排之隔的杰克。杰克点点头,使了一下眼色,在说"可以行动了,伙计!"

莉斯·斯莱特站在艾瑞克的正前方,左手拿着她那伟大的发言稿。搁在她椅子下面的是那个臭名昭著的棕色小包。艾瑞克寻思了一整天的时刻终于到了。如果这会儿他弄砸了,他甚至有可能被逐出毕业典礼大会。但是,就在他勇气动摇的时候,莉斯·斯莱特转过身来,朝着杰克·弗里曼得意地笑了笑,而他只是眨了眨眼,朝她微笑着。"混蛋杰克,"她嘟囔着,声音大得其他人都听得见。

好你个莉斯,艾瑞克心想,伸张正义的时候到了。宣誓仪式一开始,他伸手揪住了帽子上流苏的一端,轻轻地一拽。他的帽子掉到地上,他弯腰去捡。确信没有人注意到他后,他的手很快伸进口袋,取出她妹妹的宠物青蛙——克莱伦斯,然后把它扔进了装有莉斯娃娃鞋的袋子里。艾瑞克重新站了起来,这时宣誓仪式结束了。当他随大家一起坐好后,他努力地不让自己笑出声来,"一切都扯平了。"

接下来的几分钟似乎过得很慢。像往常一样,学生乐队奏起了有点儿跑调的校歌,布莱恩先生发表了几句干巴巴的讲话,伟大的时刻终于到了。莉斯·斯莱特站起身,提着她的小纸袋,走向讲台。当她经过杰克的座位时, 她向他露出了胜利的微笑, 然后跨步上前。

"大家都知道,杰克·弗里曼本来被选中来做此次发言,但是他觉得你们想听我的发言,对此我向他表示感谢。"杰克只是笑了笑。场内响起了零星的掌声。杰克回头看了艾瑞克一眼,向他做出了早已准备好的赞许手势。

"今天,我站在你们面前,"莉斯继续说道,"我的身旁带了一件宝贝。"她用手指了指那个纸袋,这时,它微微地动了动。艾瑞克觉得自己快窒息了,然而莉斯似乎没有觉察。"我将给你们展示的东西代表了我和你们在奔向未来时已经走过的和将要踏上的道路。你们应该记得这些……"

然后她演示了起来:莉斯·斯莱特的手伸进了她那棕色的小纸袋里,取出了一双娃娃鞋……一只圆鼓鼓的癞蛤蟆正蹲在其中的一只鞋里。克莱伦斯,这只癞蛤蟆发出了一声及时的鸣叫,纵身跳到了讲台上。莉斯惊呆着站在那儿,瞪大了眼睛看着那只绿色的家伙。接下来她犯了当晚最大的错误:她尖叫了起来。克莱伦斯显然被巨大的声响吓倒了,纵身跳下讲台,跳到莉斯的毕业礼袍上,消失在领口里。莉斯惊慌失措,一边撕扯着礼袍的拉链,一边连连后退。她撞到了乐队指挥的乐台后,跌倒在首席笛子手的腿上。这时的克莱伦斯一定像莉斯一样也吓坏了,猛地从袍子里跳了出来,不偏不倚正好落在二席笛子手的腿上。这时,笛子演奏手们乱成了一团,摔坏了折叠椅子,撞倒了乐台。莉斯在忙乱中正好爬进了低音鼓架下,整个架子哗的一声塌在了她的身上。

布莱恩先生仍在试图弄明白发生了什么事,这时杰克站在了讲台前。他的及时赶到恰到好处。

"谢谢你,莉斯,"杰克对着话筒大声说道,"谢谢你用那种小小的特技来帮助我。各位,放松一下,我们花了很长时间设计了这种表演。莉斯,我想大家都被我们愚弄到了。"

布莱恩先生瞪眼看着杰克,接着又转过头去看着莉斯,她仍在大号手的帮助下从鼓架下往外爬。毕业班的同学们开始大笑起来。突然,斯蒂夫和托德开始鼓起掌来,很快,全场的观众也跟着鼓起了掌。

有一位喇叭手设法逮住了克莱伦斯,走上前去把那只大蛤蟆递给了杰克。莉斯最终站了起来,努力在琢磨着发生了什么事情。看到人人都在鼓掌,她只得做了一件她觉得唯一能做的事情:对大家鞠了一躬。

"各位,难道她还没有让你们明白吗?来吧,莉斯。"杰克喊道。掌声越来越响。她走到讲台边,杰克张开双臂搂住她,低声说道,"和我站在一起,你会没事的。"然后他转向听众,认真地说道,

"这位小姐和我只是想让我们都懂得，生活不仅仅是一串串婴儿的脚步，在许多情况下我们需要做出巨大的跳跃！对吗，莉斯？"莉斯使劲地点了点头，祈祷这是正确的选择。"从今天起，你们和我正在跨出巨大的一步，我们正在跨向明天……"

说完，杰克开始了他一生中的一次重大演讲。他的声音被全场雷鸣般的掌声打断了5次。当他完成了演讲，他握住莉斯的手，他们两个再一次向台下的观众鞠躬，然后走向自己的座位。当他扶着莉斯走下台阶时，她靠近他，轻轻地问，"你为什么那么做？你本可以嘲弄我的。"

杰克露出了他标志性的微笑，说道，"哦，不，我只是在寻找一种方式，好让我们两个带着难忘的记忆离开这儿。"说完，他拥抱了一下莉斯，然后走向自己的座位，一边还想着，毕业典礼大会过后他是否要给莉斯·斯莱特一瓶可口可乐呢。

Letting Go

6

爱的放飞

I know you better
than anyone else.
I'm familiar with all of your ways.
You can't begin
to comprehend
My precious thoughts of you.
Even before you were conceived,
I ordained all of your days
with purpose.
I'll instruct you
and teach you
in the way that you should go,
Counseling you and
watching over you.
When you're discouraged or afraid,
remember I'm with you
twenty-four hours a day,
wherever you go!

LOVE,
YOUR GOD AND BEST FRIEND

—from Psalms 139:1–18; 32:8; Joshua 1:9

我比其他任何人都更了解你，

我谙悉你的方方面面。

你不会懂得我对你的珍视。

甚至在你被孕育之前，

我就特意安排了你的所有时日。

我将按照你应有的模式，

教诲你，指导你，

并且在你灰心和害怕时

关注你，忠告你。

请记住，

无论你走到哪儿，

我都将会一天24小时与你同行！

爱你的，

上帝与挚友

——摘自：《诗篇》139:1—18;32:8;《约书亚记》1:9

Friendships are the spice that makes life worth living. They give us hope and confidence to face whatever tomorrow may bring. But if we cling too tightly to those we care for, we underestimate the power of the bond. Time forges great friendships that will not wither in a season. There is something wonderful to be found in friendships that have stood the test of distance and age.

Good friends have the amazing ability to go through long times apart and then pick up right where they left off.

Trust your friendships to be enduring. Value the bonds that have been built over time. Keep investing in those relationships: call, write, visit. Above all else, believe in the commitment of caring, and trust the integrity of love. It will prove hardier than tough times and mightier than miles.

Thank you, Lord, for the friends who've blessed my life and shaped my soul.

友谊是丰富生活的调味品，它们带来希望和信

心，让我们足以应对明天发生的一切。但是如果我们苦

苦依恋于我们所关心的人，我们分明是低估了友谊的力

量。时间锻造的伟大友谊不会昙花一现。在友谊里我

们能发现某种经得起岁月和距离考验的神奇东

西。真诚的朋友能历经长久的分离而

始终不渝，再次相聚时又一

切如初。

相信你的友谊会经久不衰,珍惜历经岁月

而构筑的友谊吧。要不断地在友情的天地里投入:打个电

话,写封信,拜访拜访。最重要的是,相信关爱的承诺,信

任爱的真诚。这将证明友谊比无情的岁月更坚强,比

漫长的道路更伟大。

　　感谢你,上帝,给了为我的生命

祈福并塑造了我的灵魂的

朋友们。

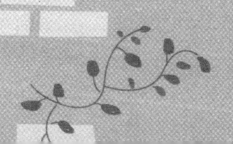

Simple pleasures of growing up together are preserved in the keepsake albums of our hearts.

—Jane Debord

一起成长的这种简简单单的快乐永存于我们心灵的纪念册。

——珍·黛博德

Their friendship was too rich, too deep for physical attraction to louse it up.

他们的友谊太纯太深，
　　不会被肉体方面的
　　　　吸引糟蹋的。

Their friendship was too rich, too deep for physical attraction to louse it up.

Best Friends

"Got one! " Teri shouted and held up the tiny shell for Rick to see. He squinted in the sunshine and was about to declare it empty when he caught a glimpse of the little legs of a hermit crab retreating into the curve of the shell. She had beaten him...just like always.

"OK, but I bet I can get five before you do! "

"You're on, loser! " Teri called back and bent over the tide pools again.

This part of the beach had always been their sanctuary. Rick tried to remember the first time he had seen her here. They were both in fourth grade, and Pacific Elementary's field trip to the ocean had been the highlight of the year. Fifty squealing eight-year-olds leaping from tide pool to tide pool, discovering new treasures at every turn. He saw her leaning over a shallow cut in one rock that held several large sea anemones. Her long, red hair nearly touched the water as she peered at the strange-looking creatures.

"If you poke your finger in them, they disappear," Rick said from behind her.

"Don't be silly," she replied without looking up. "Just 'cause I moved here from Kansas doesn't mean I don't know about sea stuff."

"No, I'm not kidding. Stick your finger in the middle, and you'll see."

Teri looked at him with narrow-eyed skepticism. "You do it first."

"OK," Rick said and squatted down next to her. "But if it sucks me in, tell the teacher so my mom and dad will know what happened to me." Teri rolled her eyes but watched closely as Rick reached into the salt water and gently poked one of the smaller creatures right in the center of its body. As soon as his finger touched its feelers, the animal balled up into a tiny knot, nearly disappearing in the sand.

"It's pulling me in," Rick screamed in mock horror, holding his finger against the animal. "Help me please!" Teri panicked, grabbed Rick by the arm, and pulled with all her weight. They both tumbled onto the sand and Rick laughed out loud. Seeing that she had been duped, she splashed a handful of water in Rick's direction.

"You're a creep!"

"I'm sorry. You just looked so scared!" He wiped the water off his face and stuck out his hand in gesture of peace, "I'm Ricky Satterfield."

"I'm Teri Graves." They shook hands and became instant friends.

Through the years, they had seen each other through losing tonsils and losing grandparents. Rick had been there for Teri when her parents divorced, and Teri had been Rick's support when his brother had nearly died as a result of a terrible motorcycle accident during his first year of college.

Some friends predicted they would end up dating,

but it just never came to pass. Rick always believed it was because their friendship was too rich, too deep for physical attraction to louse it up. So instead, they became closer than brother and sister. No one was surprised when Teri, as homecoming queen, asked Rick to be her escort. Theirs had been a story-book friendship... till now.

"Done!" Teri shouted just as Rick nabbed his final crabby victim. "I've got five too. I just didn't yell fast enough." He held out his hand as proof, and as he did, one of the crabs scurried over his palm and fell back into the surf.

"I believe you have four," Teri said with mock disapproval.

They dropped all the crabs into an empty soda cup Rick had found and sat like little children watching the crabs climb over one another trying to find a way out of their Styrofoam prison.

"Remember when we decided to take some home and start a crab farm?"

Teri grimaced, "Ohhhh, I had managed to wipe that memory from my mind."

"You were the one who said we could keep them alive in a cup. The next morning I told my mom they were just sleeping. It wasn't until they started to smell that she convinced me they were dead."

"We had a burial at sea. That I do remember." They sat in a comfortable silence for several minutes, watching the surf and thinking about the past.

"Those were good times. Sometimes I wish I could just go back and stay there," Rick finally said.

"Me too."

"But times change, huh?"

"Yeah." Teri wanted to say more but didn't know how. When she had let Rick know of her decision to attend Davidson University in North Carolina instead of Berkley with him, he hadn't handled it well.

"If you wanted to avoid me, you didn't have to pick a college on the other side of the country! " he had said with more than a little sarcasm in his voice. She had started several times to defend her choice, but somehow knew it would just add insult to injury. They were too close for logical rationales or self-defensive explanations.

They had always trusted each other's love, and this time could be no different.

"I've been thinking a lot about this fall," Rick said, poking down one of the crabs who had nearly reached the rim of the cup. "It's hard to imagine not seeing you every week."

"You're telling me," Teri said with a sigh. "Yesterday, my mother gave me the picture of us the summer we did the junior life-saving camp."

"That one with those goofy sunglasses?"

"That's it. She had it framed for me to take to Davidson and left it on my dresser. I cried like a baby when I saw it."

"You'll be fine," Rick said, placing his hand on her knee.

"And so will you," Teri said softly. Then she added, "And so will we." She slipped her hand around his, and they sat in silence again.

"Promise me you won't make any stupid decisions without calling me first," Rick said.

"Me? You're the one I'm worried about! What

about Sylvia Perkins?"

"Teri, you don't want to go there! Do I need to mention Jeff Timmons? Or Brad Henegar? Or Barry Ross?"

"OK, OK. I promise to call you before making any stupid decisions."

"And I promise to tell you not to be stupid."

"And do you promise not to quit caring just 'cause I'm three thousand miles away?"

Rick looked at Teri and then at the cup full of crabs. "There are some things you can't hold too tightly. If you try, they just die." He slowly poured the captive crabs back out into the closest tide pool where they disappeared as soon as they hit the water. "Your only choice is to let go and trust that they will be there the next time you come looking."

Teri leaned over and hugged him tightly, and he held her even tighter. As they did, they could almost feel a chapter of their lives closing as another began. They walked the beach one last time: best friends... for always.

友谊天长地久

"抓到了一个!"泰瑞喊了起来,拿着小小的贝壳给瑞克看。他在阳光下眯着眼,正想说这是个空贝壳时,却突然看见了寄生蟹的几条小腿缩进了曲形的贝壳里面。她战胜了他……总是这样。

"好的,但是我敢说我比你先抓到5只!"

"来吧,你输定了!"泰瑞接受了挑战,又弯下腰在潮水过后留下的水坑里搜寻起来。

这一片海滩是他们常去的地方,瑞克努力回忆起第一次他在这儿见到她时的情景。那时他们上四年级,太平洋小学当年让人印

象深刻的事情是组织了一次去海边的野外体验课。50个吵吵闹闹

的8岁大的孩子蹦蹦跳跳地从一个潮水坑跑向另一个潮水坑,每到

一处便搜寻着新的宝藏。他看见她弯着腰盯着一块岩石上的浅浅

裂缝,上面趴着几只大海葵。她凝视着那些模样奇特的生物,红色

的长发几乎垂到了水面。

"如果你用手指戳向它们,它们就消失了,"瑞克站在她身后

说道。

"别那么蠢," 她头也不抬地回答,"我虽然是从堪萨斯州搬

迁来的,但并不表明我对海洋生物不了解。"

"不,我不是在开玩笑,把你的手指伸到中间你就会看到。"

泰瑞用怀疑的眼光看着他。"你先试试。"

"好啊,"瑞克说着便在她的旁边蹲了下来。"不过,如果它把

我吸了进去,你得告诉老师一声,好让我的爸爸妈妈知道我发生了

什么。"泰瑞转动着眼睛,认真地看着瑞克把手伸进了咸咸的海

水,然后轻轻在一只小一点儿的海葵身体正中间戳了一下。他的手

指一碰到它的触角,这只动物便蜷起身子缩成了一小团,几乎消失在沙子里。

"它拖住我了,"瑞克假装着发出了恐惧的尖叫声,用他的手指抵着那只海葵。"快救救我!"泰瑞恐慌起来,抓住瑞克的胳膊,用尽全身力气拖住他。他们俩跌倒在沙滩上,瑞克放声大笑起来。明白自己受骗了之后,她捧起一捧水朝瑞克泼了过来。

"你讨厌!"

"对不起,你看上去真的害怕了!"他擦了擦脸上的水,伸出手摆出和平的姿势,"我叫瑞克·萨特菲尔德。"

"我叫泰瑞·格雷夫斯。"他们握了握手,立刻成了朋友。

许多年过去了,他们彼此经历了摘除扁桃体腺、痛失了祖父母等事情。当泰瑞的父母离异时,瑞克和她在一起,当瑞克的兄弟在大一年级由于一场可怕的摩托车车祸而差点丧生时,泰瑞成了他的支柱。

一些朋友预言他们将谈起恋爱,但是这样的事情从来没有发生。瑞克总是认为这是因为他们的友谊太纯太深，不会被肉体方面的吸引糟蹋的。于是他们反而变得比兄弟姐妹更亲密。当泰瑞当上校友返校会皇后而要求瑞克做她的陪伴时，别人也就不感到惊讶了。他们保持着书本上描述过的友谊……直到现在。

"好了！" 就在瑞克摁住他最后一只挣扎着的不幸小寄生蟹时，泰瑞喊了起来。"我也抓到了5只，我只是没有很快地喊出来。"他伸出手来证明他说的话时，一只寄生蟹飞快爬出他的手掌，掉进了浪花里。

"我看你只有4只，"泰瑞假装着反驳道。

瑞克找到了一个空的汽水杯，他们把所有的寄生蟹放了进去，然后像小孩子似的坐在那儿，看着寄生蟹们相互攀爬着努力寻找它们的泡沫塑料监狱之门。

"记得那时我们决定带一些回家开办一家螃蟹场的事吗？"

泰瑞做了一个鬼脸，"哦哦哦，我已经把那件事从记忆里抹去了。"

"你说我们可以把它们养在杯子里，第二天早上我告诉我的妈妈它们还在睡觉，直到它们开始发臭了我才相信妈妈说的它们已经死了。"

"我们举行了海葬,那件事我还记得。"他们平静而舒坦地坐了几分钟,注视着浪花,思考着过去。

"那是多么美好的时光啊,有时候,我希望我能回到过去,只停留在那些日子里,"瑞克最后说道。

"我也是。"

"但是时光在变啊?"

"是的。"泰瑞想再说点什么,但是不知道如何开口。当她向瑞克透露了她决定到北卡罗来纳州上戴维森大学而不是和他一起上伯克利大学时,他很是不高兴。

"如果你想回避我，也大可不必在国土的另一端选一所大学!"他的声音里带着很浓的讽刺味道。有好几次他想为自己的选择辩护,但是知道这只会是雪上加霜。对于逻辑推理或者自我辩解他们都毫不示弱。他们总是信任彼此的爱,这一次也是一样。

"对于这个秋季我一直考虑很多,"瑞克边说边用手将其中一只几乎爬到杯沿的螃蟹摁了下去。"不能每周见到你是很难想象的。"

"我知道,"泰瑞叹了口气。"昨天,我妈妈给我看了我们夏天参加三年级救生野营活动时一起照的相片。"

"戴着让人好笑的太阳镜照的那张吗?"

"是的,她把它放在相框里,让我带到戴维森,放在我的梳妆台上。当我看见它时,我像小孩子一样哭了起来。"

"你会没事的,"瑞克说着把手放在她的膝盖上。

"你也会,"泰瑞温柔地说道,然后又补充道,"我们都会没事的。"她悄悄地把手放在他的手上,他们又静静地坐在那儿。

"答应我,你不会事先不打个电话就做出一些愚蠢的决定吧。"瑞克说道。

"我? 我还担心你呢! 西尔维亚·帕金斯还好吧?"

"泰瑞,你不要去那儿!需要我提及杰夫·提蒙斯,或者布雷德·亨利加尔,或者贝利·罗斯吗?"

"好的,好的,我答应你在做出愚蠢的决定前给你打个电话。"

"我也向你保证不做傻事。"

"你保证不会因为我在3000英里之外而不关心我吗?"

瑞克看着泰瑞,又看了看装满了螃蟹的杯子。"有些东西你不能紧紧地控制住,如果你那样做,它们只会死去。"他慢慢地把捕捉到的螃蟹倒进最近的一个潮水坑里,这些小生物一到水里便消失得无影无踪。"你唯一的选择就是放手,相信下一次你来寻找时它们还会出现在那里。"

泰瑞弯下腰,紧紧地抱住了他,他也更紧搂住了她。这时,他们俨然觉得他们生命的一章结束了,而另一章又开始了。他们最后一次漫步在海滩上:最诚挚的朋友……直到永远。

chapter 7

Healing Hurts

7

抚平爱的伤口

I'm working in you to will
and act according to
My good and perfect will.
Trust in me with all your heart.
Don't rely on your own
limited understanding.
Remember, I have the advantage
of seeing the entire picture!
when you acknowledge me
in all you say and do,
I'll faithfully
direct your steps.

GUIDING YOU,
YOUR GOD OF WISDOM

—from Philippians 2:13; Proverbs 3:5–6

我在你们心里运行，
让你按照我善良而美好的
旨意实现愿望。
请全心全意地相信我，
不要依赖你自己的聪明。
记住吧，
我的优势在于纵览全局！
当你以你的言行接受了我，
我将忠实地指引你走过每一步。

引导你的
智慧之神

——摘自：《腓力比书》2：13；《箴言》3：5-6

Love is a double-edged sword. It brings the greatest joys and the greatest pains people can know. It wants to hold and nurture, to rescue and protect. This is its nature.

But moments of growth and steps toward maturity will often be taken against the pull of those we love. Don't let this fool you: Love is not the enemy. Give thanks for those who care for you and seek to guard your way. See them not as obstacles, but as opportunities to grow and love in a different way.

Be gentle as apron strings are cut and wings are tested. Be firm when the call of God on your heart leads you to places that love may find threatening or even frightening. And quietly remind your heart that someday you, too, will cling with loving arms to someone or something that deserves to fly.

Let me love those who love me with the respect I seek and the tenderness they deserve.

爱是一把双刃剑，它带来了人世间最大的欢乐

和最大的痛苦。它需要约束、培育、救助和保护——这是

它的本性。

但是成长的时刻和迈向成熟的脚步常常会受到我

们所爱的人的牵制。不要被此蒙骗：爱不是敌人。

感谢那些关心你并努力去保护你的人吧，

不要视他们为障碍，而要把他们

当做给予你成长机会

和另一种

方式的爱的人。

当裙带被剪断,奋飞的翅膀受到考验时,请温柔以

对;当心中神的召唤指引你到达了爱会受到威胁甚至恐

吓的地方时,请坚强挺立。请悄悄提醒自己,将来某一

天你也会用关爱的双臂搂住应该腾飞的某人或

某事。

让我爱那些给予我苦苦寻

找的尊重和温柔之心

的人吧。

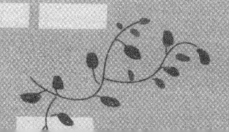

There is a path before you
that you alone can walk.
There is a purpose that you
alone can fulfill.

—Karla Dornacher

你的面前有一条你能独自走过的路，你的心中有一个你能独自完成的意愿。

——卡拉·多娜奇尔

When the college's
dean of admissions
called with a
full scholarship,
the dream turned into a nightmare.

当大学的招生办主任
打来电话，
说她获得了全额奖学金时，
这个梦想却变成了
一场噩梦。

When the college's
dean of admissions
called with a
full scholarship,
the dream turned into
a nightmare.

Picture Perfect

Cathy and her mother circled the town square one more time. At three o'clock on a Friday afternoon, parking spots were at a premium in the tiny downtown. The ride from the farm had been silent, but it was better than the alternative. Any conversation she had tried to have with her mom over the last six months had ended the same way: Cathy in tears and her mother in silence.

Thankfully, the taillights on an old blue, Chevy (an Impala, Cathy thought) signaled that whoever owned it was about to vacate his precious space. Cathy whipped around the square to get in position to grab the spot.

"We do have a speed limit in this town," her mother

said curtly. Cathy slowed down without a word. "Not like the big city where you can drive as you like, do as you please, and nobody cares."

Cathy eased the truck into the spot and turned off the engine. "You want to come in with me?"

"You go ahead. My opinion doesn't seem to count for much these days."

"Mom, please. Can't we have a truce?"

Cathy's mom was silent again. Cathy heaved a sigh and got out of the truck alone. She wished she were already at college in California and that the little town square of Highfield was far away.

No more driving two hours just to get to a mall.

No more choosing from the same two places to eat every Friday night.

No more getting recognized as "Jack and Sarah Williams's little girl" everywhere she went.

But her mother had amassed a different list. From the time Cathy had told her of the scholarship offer from Pepperdine, she had started working on it. By now it ran for several pages, but the top three were always the same.

No more safety net for friends and family to catch her if she fell.

No more dinners with the family every Sunday after church.

And, most important, no more mother to watch and pray over her every move.

"There is no way in the world that I am going to let my last child go halfway around the world to some heathen city for college. If Cleburn Community was good enough for your brother Jimmy..." Her brother had dutifully attended the closest school to the family and the farm and was well on his way to becoming a true "Highfielder". Cathy had coined the term for the folks in town who saw no reason to stray from its confining borders more than necessary. And Jimmy was happy with that. Working at the Piggly Wiggly and helping Dad at harvest time was his idea of a great life. "I might even be a manager in a few years," he had informed her at dinner one night.

For a while, Cathy thought she was the problem. There must be something wrong with her crazy notions of living in a big city far from the comforts of Highfield and home. But whenever Mr. Acuff put out the new travel magazines at his drugstore, she was the first to snatch one up. New York. Los Angeles. London. Paris. She could see herself living in any one of them. Any place with a subway, a symphony, and lots of people.

Pepperdine had been a bolt from the blue. A recruiter had sent her a brochure because of her stellar scores on the SAT.   (Even her normally stoic father had raised an eyebrow. "Top 1 percent in the country. Ain't that something?") Cathy had quietly filled out the response card and returned it. Malibu, California, seemed like an impossible dream to her, but what's wrong with a little dreaming now and then? When the college's dean of admissions called with a full scholarship, the dream turned into a nightmare.

"Absolutely not! " Her mother had pronounced with

uncommonly twisted logic: "If they are willing to let kids go for free, then it can't be much of a college. Must be pretty hard up for students." It had steadily gotten worse from there.

Cathy dropped a quarter into the parking meter, gave one more pleading look to her mother sitting stone-faced in the cab, and went alone into Bently's Photography. Mr. Bently looked up as the bell that his father's father had hung above the door rang and announced her entrance. "Well, Cathy Williams. Been waiting to show you these," Frank Bently said excitedly. "Better not let the boys around here see these, or you'll never make it out to California! "

"Are you sure you're talking about my pictures, Mr. Bently?" Cathy took a seat at the counter where countless students had sat to review their senior portraits. Mr. Bently placed a large white folder in front of her with great care.

"You look for yourself. Just don't get your fingerprints on them."

Mr. Bently had not been exaggerating: Cathy's pictures were breathtaking. Her auburn hair cascaded around her face, forming a perfect frame. And the photographer had managed to capture the expression of dreamy optimism that was the essence of her personality.

"I hope those folks in Malibu are ready for you."

"Well, Malibu seems a long ways off today."

Mr. Bently glanced out at the parked truck and nodded. "Your mom still not letting go?"

"Does everybody in this town know everything about my life?"

"This is Highfield, Cathy. People care. Just remember, your mom wanted to do the same thing herself."

Cathy stopped looking at the pictures and turned to Mr. Bently. "What did you say?"

A mischievous smile crossed Frank Bently's face. "Wait a minute." He disappeared into the back of his shop and came out with a dusty envelope.

"Came across these when I was cleaning out some files this spring. Was gonna give them to your dad to surprise your mom, but I never got around to it."

Cathy opened the folder and let out a low sigh. She had the strange sensation that she was looking at herself, but it was her mother's face smiling back at her as she had never known her: as a senior in high school. A bright, perky smile was on her lips, and she had her head cocked at an angle that almost said, "You'll never guess what all I'm going to do."

"Your mom was something. Broke every heart in town when she announced she was going to Philadelphia."

"My mother was going to Philadelphia?"

"Oh yeah. Big art school up there. Thought she might be the next Rembrandt, I guess. They were going to give her a free ride. Too bad. Her momma died just two months before she was supposed to leave."

"She never told me any of that," Cathy said in a stupor.

"Oh my goodness. I've done it now." He snatched back the pictures as though he could somehow take back what had been revealed.

"Please. May I have them?"

Mr. Bently looked out at the truck again. "I suppose they might come in handy. Eh?"

Cathy smiled and nodded, and Mr. Bently slid the yellowing folder back to her. "Good luck, Cathy. Your mom loves you a lot."

"I know that," she said looking at the folder of pictures and deciding what to do. "And the pictures look great. Thanks, Mr. Bently. The one you had on top will be perfect."

Cathy signed a form and selected the number of copies she wanted then made her way back out to the truck.

"Pictures turn out all right?" her mother asked as she shut the door.

"They were OK, but not as good as these." Cathy laid the photographs in her mother's lap.

"Oh my word," her mother said as she opened the folder and began thumbing through the pictures. "What was that crazy Frank Bently doing showing you these?"

"They're beautiful, Mom. You were a lovely girl—with a bright future."

Cathy's mom looked up from the pictures and then back toward the photography shop.

"Philadelphia is a long way from here," Cathy said softly. "Nearly as far as California."

Sarah Williams lowered her head.

"I guess I should have been able to figure out between the date of Granny Matthews's death and your graduation, but the art scholarship—why didn't you tell me?"

"Fools thought I could draw. They would have learned different."

"Maybe not. But you'll never know, will you?"

"Are you judging my choices?"

"No, Mom. Not for a minute. God gave each of us the right to make our own choices. And those who love us should respect that."

Words formed on Cathy's mom's lips, but they never made it out. As the tears came, she leaned toward her daughter and held her tightly. Cathy's tears mingled with her mother's, and they both sat hugging and crying in the cab of the truck parked in the middle of Highfield town square. When words did come, Cathy's mom began: "I just want you to be all right. I love you so much."

"I know, Mom. I love you too. And I'll be all right." After another hug, Cathy picked up one of the pictures. "Can I have one of these?"

"Sure. But if you put it up in that dorm room in Malibu, you'll have to tell the boys I'm already taken."

Cathy looked at her mom with a mixture of surprise and relief. "Oh, Momma! " And they hugged again.

"All right, let's get going. I want to show these to your father. He's probably forgotten what a good choice he made! "

They laughed together for the first time in months as Cathy backed out the truck and headed for home.

完美的照片

　　凯茜和她的母亲绕着小城的广场又转了一圈。在星期五的下午3点钟,小小商业区的停车位爆满。从农场开车来的路上她们一直保持沉默,不过这比说着话情况更好。在过去的6个月里,她试图和母亲的任何谈话都是以同样的方式而结束:凯茜泪流满面,母亲沉默不语。

　　谢天谢地,一辆旧的、蓝色的雪佛兰汽车(英帕拉,凯茜嘀咕道)的尾灯亮了,表明它的主人正准备腾出他那珍贵的车位。凯茜迅速掉转车头,准备抢占车位。

　　"这座城市有限速规定,"她的母亲冒了一句。凯茜什么话也没说，减缓了速度，"不像在大城市，你想怎么开车就怎么开车，随心所欲，没有人管。"

凯茜稳稳地将车开进了车位，关掉了引擎。"您想和我一起进去吗？"

"你先进去吧，如今我的意见似乎起不了多大作用了。"

"妈妈，请吧，难道我们不能休战吗？"

凯茜的母亲又沉默了。凯茜叹了一口气，独自走出了汽车。她多么希望她已经上了加州的大学，远离了海菲尔德这小小城市的广场。

不再开车两个小时只是为了去一趟大购物中心了。

不再在每个星期五的晚上只有两个同样地方可以选择去吃饭了。

不再每走到一处就被人们认出她是"杰克和莎拉·威廉斯的小女儿"了。

但是她的妈妈已经罗列了一份不同的清单。自从凯茜告诉她获得了佩波戴恩大学的奖学金之后，她就开始准备这份清单了。现在,这份清单长达几页纸了,但是头三条总是一样。

如果她摔倒了,不再有朋友和家人的安全网保护着她了。

每个星期天做完祷告后,不再能够和家人一起共进晚餐了。

最重要的是,不再有妈妈在身边关注着她的一举一动,为她祈祷了。

"在这个世界上,我没有理由要让我的最小一个孩子绕过大半个地球到某个陌生的城市去读大学。如果克莱博恩社区大学对于你兄弟吉米来说足够好的话……"她的兄弟老老实实地就读于离家庭和农场最近的学校,正在稳稳当当地成为一名真正的"海菲尔德人"。凯茜曾经为城里那些觉得没有任何必要离开自己生活圈子的人们生造了这个词。吉米似乎对这个称呼很满意,平时在皮格力·威格力超市上班,农忙时帮助父亲干活便是他理想中的伟大生活。"几年之后我或许能够当一名经理,"曾经有一天晚上他在餐桌上对她说过这样的话。

有一段时间,凯茜觉得自己出了毛病,她那想去大城市而远离舒适家庭和海菲尔德的疯狂想法一定有点问题。然而,每当阿克尤夫先生在他的药店里摆出新的旅行杂志时,她总是第一次抢着去看。纽约、洛杉矶、伦敦、巴黎,她能够想象着自己生活在其中的任何一个,那些有地铁、交响乐和很多人的地方。

佩波戴恩曾经是一个晴天霹雳。一位招生人员因为看到了她的学术能力测试的成绩而给她发了一本招生简章(她那一向沉着的父亲也扬起了眉毛,"全国百分之一的比例,是不是那回事?")凯茜悄悄地填好回执卡,寄了回去。对她来说,加州的马利布海滩似乎是一件不可能实现的梦想,但是时不时来一点小小的梦想又有什么不可以呢?当大学的招生办主任打来电话,说她获得了全额奖学金时,这个梦想却变成了一场噩梦。

"绝对不行!"她的妈妈用异于寻常的逻辑发话道,"如果他

们希望让孩子们免费上大学,这就不可能是一所好大学,一定对学

生很苛刻。"情况从那时开始变得更糟糕了。

　　凯茜把一个25美分的硬币扔进了停车计费器,再一次用恳求

的眼光看了一眼坐在车中的铁青着脸的母亲,独自走进了本特利

照相馆。本特利先生听到他祖父挂在门上的铃铛响了,抬起头示意

她进去。"啊,凯茜·威廉斯,一直在等你来看这些东西呢,"弗兰

克·本特利激动地说道。"最好不要让周围的男孩子们看到这些,

否则你永远也去不了加州!"

　　"您是在说我的照片吗,本特利先生?"凯茜在柜台旁边的一

个座位上坐下,曾经有数不清的学生坐在那儿浏览他们的毕业照。

本特利先生小心翼翼地把一个大大的白色相册放到她面前。

　　"你自己看看吧,不要把手印弄到上面。"

抚 平 爱 的 伤 口

本特利先生没有夸张:凯茜的照片真是漂亮极了。她褐色的头发飘逸在脸的四周,勾勒出一副完美的轮廓。摄影师成功地捕捉到了一种梦幻般的乐观神情,这是她真实的性格。

"我希望马利布的人们已经为你准备好了。"

"哎,马利布在今天看来似乎还是遥远的事情。"

本特利先生朝停车场上的汽车望了一眼,点了点头。"你的妈妈还不让你走吗?"

"难道这个小镇里的每个人都了解我生活的一切事情吗?"

"这是海菲尔德,凯茜。人们关心别人,你得记住,你的母亲自己也一样。"

凯茜停止了看照片,转向本特利先生,"您说什么呀?"

弗兰克·本特利的脸上滑过一丝诡异的微笑,"稍等一等,"他消失在店的后面,拿出一个尘封的信封。

"这是今年春天我在清理材料时无意间发现的,准备把它们送给你的父亲,好让你的母亲惊喜一场,但是我却一直没能抽出时间送过去。"

凯茜打开相册,发出了轻轻的叹息声。她有一种奇怪的感觉,觉得她正在看着她自己,但这是她母亲的脸庞,正在微笑着看着她,好像她从来都不认识她:一名高三的学生。她的嘴角流露出一种开朗而神气的微笑,她的头部朝着一定的角度倾斜着,似乎在说,"你永远也猜不透我要干的一切事情。"

"你的妈妈曾是个引人注目的人,当她宣布她准备去费城时,镇上每个人都很伤心。"

"我的母亲准备去费城?"

"啊,是的,上那儿的一所很大的艺术学校,每个人都认为她会成为伦勃朗第二,我猜测。他们准备让她免费乘车去那儿。不幸的是,就在她准备出发的两个月之前,她的妈妈去世了。"

"她从来没有告诉过我任何关于此类的事情,"凯茜茫然地说道。

"哦,天哪,我把它说了出来。"他抢回照片,好像他多少能够收回一些被泄露了的秘密似的。

"求求您,我可以拥有它们吗?"

本特利先生又一次朝外面看了看那辆汽车,"我想它们或许会用得上的,嗯?"

凯茜笑了,点了点头。本特利先生把发黄的相册递给了她,"祝你好运,凯茜,你的妈妈非常爱你。"

"这我知道," 她说着并看了看相册, 心里知道该怎么做了。"这些照片看上去太棒了,谢谢您,本特利先生,您放在上面的那张将是最完美的。"

凯茜填了一张表,写下了她所需要的相片的号码,然后回到车上。

"照片都洗好了吗?" 她的母亲关上车门,说道。

"它们洗得很好,但是没有这些好。"凯茜把那些相片放在她的膝盖上。

"哎呀," 她的母亲打开相册时叫了一声,然后开始翻看相片。"那个发疯的弗兰克·本特利给你看这些东西干什么呀?"

完 美 的 照 片

"它们很漂亮,妈妈,你是一位可爱的姑娘——拥有光明的前途。"

凯茜的母亲不再看照片,她抬起头来,然后回头望着照相馆。

"费城离这儿很遥远," 凯茜轻声地说道,"和加州差不多一样远。"

莎拉·威廉斯低下了头。

"我想我应该能够理解马修斯外祖母的去世与您的毕业之间的关系,可是那笔艺术奖学金——为什么您以前不告诉我?"

"傻瓜才认为我会画画,如果我去了那儿,他们就会知道了。"

"也许不会吧,但是不去您也不会知道,不是吗?"

"你是在审判我的选择吗?"

"不是,妈妈,根本不是。上帝给了我们每个人做出自我选择的权利,那些爱我们的人应该尊重这种选择。"

话到了凯茜母亲的嘴边,但是没有说出来,眼泪流了下来,她靠近女儿,紧紧地搂住了她。在停泊在海菲尔德城市广场中心的汽车里,这一对母女就这样搂着、哭泣着坐在汽车里,泪水混成了一片。话终于来了,凯茜的妈妈开口道:"我只不过想让你平平安安的,我太爱你了。"

"我知道,妈妈,我也爱你,我会平平安安的。"她们再次地拥抱之后,凯茜拿出其中的一张照片,"我能拿走一张吗?"

"可以,但是如果你把它挂在马利布的宿舍里,你一定要告诉男生们我已经结婚了。"

凯茜看着妈妈,表情里混合着惊讶和宽慰,"哦,妈妈!"她们又一次拥抱在一起。

"好的,我们出发吧,我想把这些给你的父亲看看,他可能忘了,他做出了一个多么好的选择!"

几个月来,她们第一次在一起哈哈大笑着。凯茜把汽车掉了个头,踏上了回家的路。